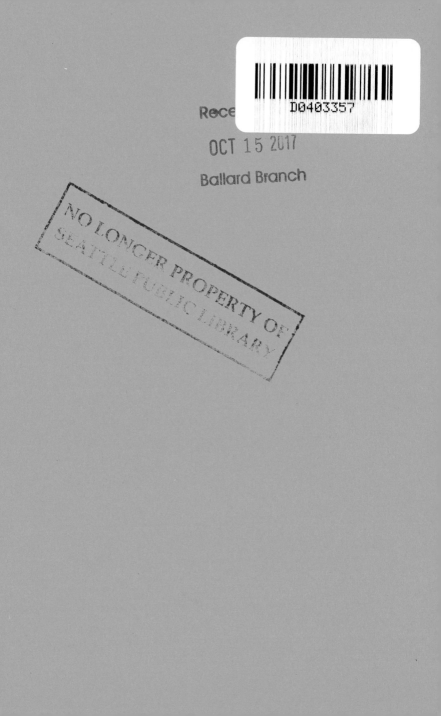

BOOK II

The Shanghai Incident

Master DIPLEXITO and Mr. SCANT

The Shanghai Incident

Bryan Methods

CAROLRHODA BOOKS
MINNEAPOLIS

Carolrhoda Books
A division of Lerner Publishing Group, Inc.
241 First Avenue North
Minneapolis, MN 55401 USA

For reading levels and more information, look up this title at www.lernerbooks.com.

Additional image: © iStockphoto.com/Roberto A Sanchez (paper background).

Main body text set in Bembo Std regular 12.5/17.
Typeface provided by Monotype Typography.

Library of Congress Cataloging-in-Publication Data

Names: Methods, Bryan, author.
Title: The Shanghai incident / Bryan Methods.
Description: Minneapolis : Carolrhoda Books, [2017] | Series: Master Diplexito and
    Mr. Scant ; book 2 | Summary: In the early 1900s, an English schoolboy and his
    criminal mastermind butler travel to Paris and then race to Shanghai to solve a
    dangerous kidnappng case and unravel a plot to attack the child emperor of China.
    | Description based on print version record and CIP data provided by publisher;
    resource not viewed.
Identifiers: LCCN 2016036267 (print) | LCCN 2017011591 (ebook) |
    ISBN 9781512448573 (eb pdf) | ISBN 9781512405804 (lb : alk. paper)
Subjects: | CYAC: Robbers and outlaws—Fiction. | Apprentices—Fiction.
    | Vigilantes—Fiction. | Missing children—Fiction. | Kidnapping—
    Fiction. | Shanghai (China)—History—20th century—Fiction. | China—
    History—1861–1912—Fiction.
Classification: LCC PZ7.1.M49 (ebook) | LCC PZ7.1.M49 Sh 2017 (print) | DDC
    [Fic]—dc23

LC record available at https://lccn.loc.gov/2016036267

Manufactured in the United States of America
1-39235-21112-3/27/2017

For my family, English
and Chinese alike. Here's
to many more happy,
delicious dinners!

Prologue

Mr. Scant peered around the wall of the gazebo, I peered around Mr. Scant, and the strange little urchin peered around me. Fortunately, our hiding place was shadowy enough that the two men didn't spot us. Besides, they were busy enjoying their cigarettes and telling jokes in French, presumably bawdy ones; from what I gathered, all French jokes were bawdy. Mr. Scant drew back, so I did the same, pulling the boy into the shadows with me.

"What are they doing there?" I whispered to Mr. Scant.

"Guarding the door," Mr. Scant rumbled, his voice so low I could only just hear the words.

"Why would they need to guard the door to a gallery?"

"Why, indeed?" Mr. Scant said, glancing down at the long-haired boy who had led us here. "It seems your little friend thinks we should have a look inside."

Meeting Mr. Scant's eye, the child gestured toward the door and said in his small voice, "Julien . . . j'pense qu'il est . . ."

I risked another glimpse. "Is that one of those Maxim guns he has?" One of the men was huge and obviously very strong, because he was holding a very big gun. The other one was there simply to hold the chain of bullets but had his own rifle on his back. It was not a very heartening sight.

"A Hotchkiss," said Mr. Scant. "Though no matter who makes a gun, its effect on your general health and well-being will be much the same. On the other hand, if he thinks he can heft that monster and fire it with any accuracy, his poor judgment will be to our advantage. Let's hope this is the only obstacle that stands between us and Reggie."

"Do you think we'll find him inside?"

"If I know my brother, he's gotten himself in hot water. It would be wise to make sure."

"Should we find a window or something to look in through?"

"What do *you* think, Master Oliver?"

I paused. "I . . . suppose even if we look in, we won't be sure unless we check everywhere. That means we need to be able to get inside. Should we try to sneak in somewhere else?"

"I would prefer to deal with these two now, if that's all the same to you, Master Oliver. Best not to risk their overhearing our investigations and catching us by surprise if we sneak in. And, well, if I find out something has happened to my brother, I'll have difficulty restraining myself."

Mr. Scant had raised his claw. There was an ominous quality to the way the long, sharp blades caught the dim evening light.

I licked my dry lips. "I suppose, for their sake, we'd better deal with them now, then. Is it going to be that easy?"

"I shouldn't think it will be especially difficult. I shall approach from the side, and we'll see how quickly he can turn that great gun of his around."

"What should I do?"

"Make sure your little vagabond friend stays exactly where he is. And if they shoot me, well, I suppose that will distract them long enough for you to bop them on the head and have a look around yourself. On your way out, I would be grateful if you could pick up whatever pieces of me are left."

I wasn't sure if this was Mr. Scant's idea of a joke. He wasn't really the joking sort. So I nodded and put my hands close enough to the French boy's shoulders that I could grab him if he did anything unexpected, yet without having to actually touch his jacket.

Mr. Scant cycled the blades of his claw to ensure they were all moving as expected. His maintenance routine remained meticulous no matter where in the world he was. Then he gave me a nod before jumping up to scale the wall. I fought the compulsion to peer around at the guards, and thankfully the boy just watched the place where Mr. Scant had vanished, as though afraid we would never see him again.

It was about twenty seconds later that we heard the great roar of the big gun—for only half a second before, abruptly, it stopped.

I

La Gioconda

"Do you think you could steal it?"

Mr. Scant raised an eyebrow at me. "For what reason, Master Oliver?"

"I'm just curious."

Mr. Scant regarded the small painting again. The *Mona Lisa* looked back with the placid expression of one with no eyebrows to raise. "Anyone can steal anything that does not belong to them at any time."

"You know what I mean," I said, as we turned away to let the next visitors look at the ordinary but apparently well-known painting. "Could you steal it without getting caught?"

"I would like to think I would manage. The Louvre is too large to guard perfectly."

I smiled. "Maybe, but Dr. Mikolaitis says this one's special. Maybe it has special protection."

"I can see no special security in place," Mr. Scant replied, after a thoughtful look about the gallery. "Of course, one could not simply lift it off the wall with so many patrons watching. Best, I would think, to come on a day when the museum is closed to the public and pose as an employee. Those smocks they wear would be useful for concealing a small painting, and with so many staff members, I cannot imagine anyone would question an unfamiliar face. So it would be a matter of procuring the smock and choosing a suitable day."

I smiled. "Maybe we should stop talking about this. You might give someone an idea."

Even though we were in Paris, it was obvious some in the crowd understood our English. I met the eye of a swarthy man with a pointed mustache who had been listening with great interest. I tried not to laugh as he pulled his hat down over his face and shuffled away, embarrassed.

We made our way to the nearby Café Mollien, one of the Louvre's grand cafeterias, where Mr. Scant's staunch ally Dr. Mikolaitis was waiting for us with a small cup of coffee, looking quite at home in the fashionable style of dress he had adopted for the trip. For the past four months or so, Dr. Mikolaitis had been employed as my tutor, and he was in his element here in France. He wore a gray jacket and a shirt with no necktie, and I felt sure that passersby who noticed his scarred face and well-tailored clothes assumed he was one of those eccentric modern artists that went on dangerous adventures and were always in the newspapers for doing something outrageous. He stood to greet us.

"Did you see *La Gioconda*'s famous smile?" he asked, the *Mona Lisa*'s original Italian name sounding strangely impressive in his Lithuanian accent.

"Yes," I replied. "Mr. Scant says he could steal it."

Dr. Mikolaitis smiled. "Perhaps the scandal that followed would give her the fame she deserves. You know, she hung in the bedroom of Napoleon himself?"

"No wonder she looks like she's seen something funny," I said.

Mr. Scant had quietly ordered some refreshments for us as he pushed my chair in behind me. Now he sat down with a sense of urgency. "What of the target?" he asked.

"He took the bait," said Dr. Mikolaitis, grinning like a tiger. "He's frightened and alone. Since the Lice scattered, he hasn't heard from a single one of them.

He almost wept with happiness when he saw me. He believes I'm still one of them, of course."

Lice was Dr. Mikolaitis's sobriquet for the members of the Woodhouselee Society, the shadowy cabal he had been forced to join, only to work with Mr. Scant to undermine them.

Mr. Scant did not look amused. "And the probability that it's all a trap and he's not as idiotic as he seems?"

"I would say low. But he could be the greatest actor of his age. Who can say?"

The waiter arrived with our tea, and Mr. Scant watched him pour it critically. When the tea was served and the waiter had withdrawn, Mr. Scant added cream and sugar to mine, just the way I liked it. Even here, he wore his white valet's gloves, oddly mismatched with his simple gray jacket.

"Did you find out where he keeps his hoard?" asked Mr. Scant.

"Where else? Under the bed. Fafnir with his treasure, only . . . this time less a fearsome dragon than a fat, bald little man."

"We should recover it with all haste," Mr. Scant said. "Do you think he will know anything of young Miss Gaunt?"

"Probably not. But it doesn't hurt to ask, hmm?"

In the months since we rescued Mr. Scant's brother from the Woodhouselee Society, we had devoted all the time we could to finding Mr. Scant's niece, Elspeth Gaunt. She had appeared to help us in our battle against the Society, but then disappeared as quickly as she came, and there had been no word from her since. Tracking her down was proving more difficult than expected.

"I hope we find her soon," I said.

"I begin to think this girl does not want to be found," said Dr. Mikolaitis.

"Reggie's debt complicates things," said Mr. Scant. "Nobody has come for the money, so perhaps Elspeth herself is working to repay it."

"And where is the esteemed Mr. Gaunt?" asked Dr. Mikolaitis. "I thought he was joining us."

"He slept in, as usual," said Mr. Scant. "I told him to meet us here. If he doesn't appear, we won't wait. He'll catch up with us when we meet the Scotland Yard contact."

Dr. Mikolaitis sat back, crossing his arms without putting down his tiny coffee cup. "You know, nobody has explained all this to me properly. This niece of yours is the girl we met at the Cobham Mausoleum?"

"Yes," said Mr. Scant. "My niece, Elspeth Gaunt. *Gaunt* rather than *Scant* because she was born after Reggie changed his name. While Reggie was working for the Society, we believed she was studying mathematics in a college here in Paris, with the Society guarding her closely, to keep Reggie in line. But when we saw her in Cobham, she had evidently learned more than mathematics."

"She could really fight!" I said. "That pretty Chinese girl too, Miss Cai. They were both amazing."

Mr. Scant nodded. "They had some skill. But where China comes into this is unclear. We believe Reggie's debt was transferred to a Chinese secret society known as the Tri-Loom, so even though the Woodhouselee Society has crumbled, that debt persists. This could mean that the Tri-Loom is controlling Elspeth's actions and enforcing payments—and she may be more in need of assistance than she implied."

"But when we saw Elspeth and that other girl, they were working *against* the Society," I said. "They helped us catch Mr. and Mrs. Binns and handed them over to Scotland Yard and everything!"

Mr. Scant took a thoughtful sip of his tea. "Indeed.

A number of mysteries remain. Perhaps Elspeth is working to thwart the Tri-Loom. I would prefer to believe that, and it's what the other young woman, Miss Cai, suggested. But from all available evidence, this Tri-Loom is a much more powerful organization than the Woodhouselee Society ever was."

"Don't expect to get much out of today's little mole man," Dr. Mikolaitis said, looking down at his cup and shaking it as though that would dislodge some more coffee. "For my part, I'm happy to be liberating works the Society stole and restoring them to the people."

Mr. Scant gave a noncommittal grunt, then asked, "Master Oliver, would you like an éclair?"

After the pot of tea was finished and the éclair thoroughly enjoyed, we gave up on the arrival of Mr. Scant's brother Reginald—or Uncle Reggie, as I had grown to call him. Dr. Mikolaitis took us on a short tour through the Louvre, mostly showing us paintings of Napoleon, a man Dr. Mikolaitis seemed to think was at once the most admirable and most loathsome person ever born. At the end of the short tour, Dr. Mikolaitis told us our target was waiting up ahead, and that Mr. Scant and I ought to keep our distance.

"What's his name?" I asked.

"Antoine Bernard," said Dr. Mikolaitis. "A plain name for a plain man. He was my tutor when I was a student, and perhaps, in his way, he really believed that sending me to the Lice would improve my life. He thinks the world will consider him a reincarnation of the Unknown Philosopher, but not one original thought has ever passed through his head. That's him, there by the Delacroix. If you stay here, you ought to be able to hear what we say. We will speak in English."

A small man in a bowler hat and a coat that looked too hot to wear indoors loitered under a painting of a sickly-looking Mr. Chopin, the composer. The man looked up at Dr. Mikolaitis in irritation when he approached.

"You kept me waiting," he said, in such a thick French accent that I thought he said *wetting*.

"I beg your pardon," said Dr. Mikolaitis, his own Lithuanian accent mild by comparison. "I had to be sure I was not followed."

The small man's eyes widened. "We are safe, yes?"

"Quite safe. What have you heard?"

"Nothing, not a peep. The so-called 'brothers' here pretend they don't know me. 'We have never heard of this Woodhouselee.' After today, I am inclined to do the same."

"Nobody else sent word from England?"

"Only you," the small man said with a sneer. "So is it true? Is it all over?"

"Nothing is over," said Dr. Mikolaitis, fixing the other man with a serious glance. He was a good actor. "It is only changing its form. The pieces are scattered but still exist. If you want proof, well, I am here."

"Why did that fool of all fools Binns have to get himself arrested?"

"Too boastful," said Dr. Mikolaitis. "Too fond of spectacle."

The little Frenchman snorted. "It looks suspicious, us standing here too long. Shall we go to a café?"

"I don't want to risk being overheard. I seem to recall you live not so far from here."

"Hmm. Then let's go."

We followed at a safe distance as Monsieur Bernard led Dr. Mikolaitis out of the Louvre and toward the river Seine. Mr. Scant had a preternatural sense for tailing a person. He always seemed to know when Monsieur Bernard was about to look around and the speed at which to walk in order to see what turn the men would take next. Once we had moved away from the crowds and into the broad Parisian streets, Mr. Scant was more cautious, often signaling that we should pause behind trees or restaurant signs. He used his old, wide-brimmed hat to hide his face whenever he thought that Monsieur Bernard might look back. I tried to do the same with my cap while I followed precisely in Mr. Scant's footsteps, attempting to emulate his silent, catlike gait.

It became easier to follow the two men when we reached narrower side streets, so Mr. Scant closed the distance between us and them until we could hear what the two men were saying. Dr. Mikolaitis was filling Monsieur Bernard in on the situation in England, and I enjoyed hearing him telling the lie Mr. Scant had carefully crafted: "The Society collapsed when Scotland Yard found out Binns was the Ruminating Claw."

"That imbecile," said Monsieur Bernard.

Dr. Mikolaitis nodded. "There was no danger of other members being exposed, but it became an embarrassment. That doesn't mean those behind Binns, with the real power, have vanished."

"Yes, yes, but what does it mean for *me?*"

Monsieur Bernard asked. "For France, and for me?"

"That's what I'm here to discover. Once I've talked to you and the other big players."

The little man looked flattered by that and nodded. Then he produced a key and opened the door of a slightly run-down old townhouse. As the two disappeared inside, Mr. Scant gave me a little push, and we hurried after them. The door had shut behind the men, so Mr. Scant knelt down, while I brought out his lock-picking set.

I examined the size of the lock and remembered what Mr. Scant had taught me. "Picks two and seven?" I asked, already taking them out.

"You're learning," said Mr. Scant, with the tiniest hint of approval. "We're in a hurry, so I'll do this one, but we'll have you practice on the next."

The lock turned before Mr. Scant had even finished speaking, and he pushed the door open silently. Inside, we could see at once that this was not a single residence; there were a number of different doors, and then stairs leading upward. There was also a small door marked *Service*, and it was to this that Mr. Scant turned after listening intently for a few moments. The door was not locked, and we found another small staircase on the other side of it.

Mr. Scant stopped on the first step, listening again.

"What is it?" I asked.

"He's angry," said Mr. Scant. Before waiting for a reply, he dashed up the four flights of steps leading to the little apartment. I did my best to keep pace and caught up with Mr. Scant just as he barged his way through the single door at the top of the steps. Following in his wake, I rushed into the messy, dirty entrance hall of a small Parisian apartment, where overcoats, old newspapers, and the moldy ends of baguettes were strewn everywhere. The smell of rotting vegetables made me cover my nose, but there was no time to stop—we ran straight toward the raised voices Mr. Scant had been able to hear from all the way downstairs.

"The *right friends*, you say!" Monsieur Bernard was shouting, incredulous. "You come here to steal my treasures, and you tell me we need to keep the right friends?"

I couldn't see the men, but they must have been standing in front of a bright lamp, for their shadows fell upon the wall of a room at the end of the corridor. Monsieur Bernard was pointing his finger up at Dr. Mikolaitis's nose, while the doctor held his hands up, protesting his innocence.

"I'm not here to steal anything from you," said Dr. Mikolaitis.

"Of course you would say that. Too bad for you the boy came before you did. He told me everything you'd done, you traitor. You cowardly turncoat! Oh yes, I know all about your little game. What you did. You and the real Claw, you destroyed the Society! But the boy, ah, he's bringing a new Society together, here in France. Stronger than it ever was with idiots like his parents in charge. Imbecile Englishmen, always preening in front of the mirror, so they never see when're stabbed in the back."

I looked at Mr. Scant urgently, but he held up his hand. "Let him speak," he whispered, just on the edge of my hearing.

"What boy?" said Dr. Mikolaitis.

"What boy do you think?" Monsieur Bernard said, stalking away from Dr. Mikolaitis. "The Binns boy. The new *maître*. The new head of the sphinx. And he'll reward me well for doing this to the man who betrayed his parents."

"Let's not—" Dr. Mikolaitis began, starting toward the smaller man, but without warning, a gunshot rang out, and Dr. Mikolaitis's shadow twisted before dropping to the ground.

I looked at Mr. Scant wide-eyed, and he grabbed my arm. "Remember what I taught you about guns," he hissed.

"Make them aim high and hit them low," I said, a recitation from a long and painful lesson—but Mr. Scant was already hurling himself into the room, while Dr. Mikolaitis's shadow had fallen completely out of view.

II

A New Society

Mr. Scant was in the air. As I darted in after him, I saw—as if in a frozen moment—that he had leapt high, the rodent of a man looking at him with wide eyes while the barrel of the pistol still breathed out a rivulet of smoke. Mr. Scant had ensured the gun was aimed upward, and the next part was up to me.

"Hit them low," I repeated to myself. Monsieur Bernard was a small man, about my height, but with a much bigger belly. I did the only thing I could think of, launching myself at him in a clumsy sort of rugby tackle. I probably wouldn't have been able to knock down most adults, but Monsieur Bernard was taken by surprise and crashed to the floor, with me falling hard onto his rib cage.

The next thing I knew, Mr. Scant was upon us,

pulling me away with his left hand while the claw on the right flashed out, two of the blades on his fingers digging into the floorboards on either side of Monsieur Bernard's neck. Then, in practiced motions, Mr. Scant grabbed the man's wrist and twisted it in such a way that forced Bernard to roll onto his belly. Ignoring the Frenchman's cry of pain, Mr. Scant then pressed his knee into the small of the other man's back.

"Did I do the right thing?" I asked, as I got out of the way.

"Tripping him would have been . . . more elegant, Master Oliver. Now help Mykolas."

My eyes widened as I remembered Dr. Mikolaitis. I rushed over and was relieved to see him smile grimly.

"I'm alright," he told me. "Well, not alright, I'm bleeding profusely. Come, put pressure here."

After only a moment's hesitation, I pushed my fingers down on Dr. Mikolaitis's shoulder, which made him grunt. His fine new clothes were blackened all around the gunshot wound.

"Unhand me, filthy cretin!" Monsieur Bernard yelled from the floor, his face pushed into the dirty carpet. Mr. Scant ignored him.

"Pass me that vodka, lad," said Dr. Mikolaitis. "The vodka's the clear one."

He poured the liquid over his wound before taking a gulp for himself, then gritted his teeth as he slowly took off his jacket. "Bring me a sheet or something, for a bandage. Try to find something clean."

This was no easy task. Many things in Monsieur Bernard's apartment may have started off as white but now all were a sickly gray. I found a pillowcase that appeared to have been laundered relatively recently, used a letter opener to cut the seams, and then tore it open. Dr. Mikolaitis had peeled off his shirt, and he took the pillowcase with a nod of thanks.

"Will you be alright?" I asked.

"Most likely, though who knows?" said the doctor. "It may get infected, and I will die a painful death. But I should say I'm lucky. He shot me in the shoulder so he could gloat before he shot me again."

"Yes, I wanted to gloat!" shouted Monsieur Bernard. "And I would be gloating now if not for your nasty friends."

"Perhaps we should shoot you in the shoulder too and see how well you gloat then," rumbled Mr. Scant, hauling the man to his feet.

"Ha! Go ahead, see if I care. Traitorous dogs."

"Oh, that's very rich from someone whose mother won Best in Show," Dr. Mikolaitis shot back, to a cry of outrage from Monsieur Bernard.

"Should we take you to a hospital?" I asked.

"No, it's only a small amount of excruciating pain," Dr. Mikolaitis replied. "It will pass. I'll treat myself when we finish here. I am a doctor, after all."

"Aren't you the wrong sort of doctor?" I asked.

"Well, you could put it like that. I am a doctor of theology who also happens to know how to stitch himself up. It's been useful over the years. Now press this down so I can tie it properly."

Mr. Scant pushed Monsieur Bernard down on a wooden chair and bound the man's arms and legs to it with one of the lengths of rope he always seemed to carry around.

"I have an itch on my nose," the Frenchman complained.

"Bear with it," Mr. Scant said.

With a grunt, Dr. Mikolaitis got to his feet and went to join Mr. Scant. He appeared to be ignoring how rapidly the improvised bandage had soaked through. Uneasily, I went to join them.

"So, the Binns boy came to see you?" said Dr. Mikolaitis. "What did he tell you?"

"Why should I answer?" asked Monsieur Bernard. Then he met Dr. Mikolaitis's eye and seemed to instantly reconsider his position. "I–I'm sorry. He . . . means to use this disarray his idiot father made in England to make a new Society here in Paris, one that will actually act on the ideals his father pretended he admired. No more play. A Society to really change the world."

Mr. Scant looked unconvinced. "Why would the old *maîtres* support the son of an idiot? Why do you?"

"Ah, perhaps you have never met the boy," Monsieur Bernard said. "He is different. He believes. And he makes you believe."

Mr. Scant looked at Dr. Mikolaitis. "What do you think his chances are?"

"I doubt he has any chance at all," Dr. Mikolaitis said. "The *maîtres* will all want to lead the new Society themselves. Not listen to some upstart English boy."

Mr. Scant nodded. Then he looked back to Monsieur Bernard and said, "We are looking for Elspeth Gaunt. Do you know the name?"

Monsieur Bernard said nothing for a moment. Then he muttered, "This name means nothing to me."

"She was studying mathematics at the *École normale supérieure*," Mr. Scant said. "Her father was in debt to the Woodhouselee Society, and she was here under the supervision of the local members."

"I know nothing about it."

"Who would?"

"Why would I know this?" Monsieur Bernard sputtered. "And why would I tell you if I did? What does it matter now, anyway? If you know where she is, go and fetch her."

Mr. Scant persevered. "Before we brought Binns to justice—"

"Ha!"

"—it seems the debt was taken on by the Tri-Loom."

"The Tri-Loom? Ha, and I thought your problem was the Binns boy. If you start to—how do you say?—bark up that tree, you'll disappear before the boy even gets to you."

Mr. Scant let out a deep breath. When Mr. Scant sighed, it sounded older and wearier than any normal sigh, heavy like an ancient tree finally toppled by a storm. "To whom do we need to speak?"

"There is nobody to speak with! Binns, he was the only one the Tri-Loom dealt with, and even

then, they would send for him, not the ot̲
around. You don't know what you're dealing
Secret societies are one thing. Crime syndicates are
completely different. You don't understand that? Go
find out what happens if you start asking the wrong
questions."

Dr. Mikolaitis had begun to sway, and his face
was looking disturbingly pale.

"Mr. Scant, I think we need to do something
about Dr. Mikolaitis," I said.

Mr. Scant looked agitated, but Dr. Mikolaitis
reluctantly nodded. Mr. Scant adjusted his cap and
leaned forward so that his face, grimmer than any
reaper's, was inches from Monsieur Bernard's. "We'll
be taking back everything you stole, and if I find you
kept anything from us, we will return for it."

When Monsieur Bernard turned his face away
defiantly, Mr. Scant pulled out a sack that had been
hanging from his belt and gave it to me. "Get everything shiny that's under his bed. Take care not to
touch anything else. You'll likely regret it."

"And put it all in this sack?"

"What else would it be for?" Mr. Scant snapped,
then swept past me to tend to his old friend. I hurried into the dingy bedroom, which was every bit

as disgusting as I expected. Traces of old meat and bread had turned the same green color, while empty bottles lay where they had been dropped. Under the bed, between piles of clothes and rags that I tried to pretend I hadn't seen moving slightly, sat a neat wooden cigar box. I pulled it out and chanced a look within. So many jewels and gold chains had been stuffed inside that it was hard to close the lid again.

I hurried out, holding the box up demonstrably, which made Monsieur Bernard snarl. "You're making some bad enemies, boy."

"If they're all like you, I don't think they'll be a problem for Mr. Scant."

"Your precious butler won't be able to save you forever."

"He's not just our butler. He's my father's valet."

Mr. Scant had brought Dr. Mikolaitis to his feet, so I hurried over to let the injured man lean on me as Mr. Scant took the cigar box. Then he looked at Monsieur Bernard and leaned so close to him that I thought Mr. Scant's thick eyebrows would brush the other man's skin. "We are taking back your baubles and trinkets, monsieur. Scotland Yard will see them restored to their rightful owners."

The Frenchman's round face twitched as Mr. Scant stepped away from him. "You can't just leave me here!"

"You are of course a popular and well-regarded man," Mr. Scant said as he took Dr. Mikolaitis's weight from me again. "Someone will no doubt be along to visit you soon. I'm sure they will be happy to release you."

"Untie me at once!"

"I'm sorry, I have to support my friend. The one you shot."

With that, we left behind the rants of Monsieur Bernard and his squalid little apartment. I didn't look back, and felt somewhat grateful I couldn't understand the stream of French profanity that followed us.

"What if nobody *does* come for him?" I asked, as we eased Dr. Mikolaitis down the stairs. To my surprise, it was the doctor who answered.

"Lice are not so easy to kill."

Ignoring all objections, Mr. Scant took Dr. Mikolaitis to the nearest main road, where I managed to wave down a hansom cab to take us to a hospital. Dr. Mikolaitis put on a remarkable show of being in perfect health as he stepped into the cab, so as not to give the driver any cause for alarm, but by the time we got to our destination, he was paler than any of the sculptures from the Louvre. The driver apparently wasn't at all upset that he'd been tricked into transporting an injured man, and helped us take the good doctor inside.

"What shall we do now?" I asked Mr. Scant as we left the hospital, once Dr. Mikolaitis was safely admitted.

"Reggie will be meeting with this mystery man from Scotland Yard at three o'clock," said Mr. Scant. "We mustn't be late."

The helpful driver had waited for us, so Mr. Scant asked him to take us on to Notre Dame. When we arrived in front of the western façade of the famous cathedral, the scene was oddly still for a Sunday afternoon. There was nobody to be seen but a man riding his bicycle back and forth in front of the cathedral's closed wooden doors and two old men in caps pointing walking sticks at faint marks on the surrounding walls, perhaps made by last year's flood.

"Where's Uncle Reggie?" I asked.

"I wish I knew," Mr. Scant rumbled.

We waited in an inconspicuous spot by the wall overlooking the river Seine, but as time went by, it became increasingly evident that Uncle Reggie was not going to appear. The two old men shuffled off somewhere, and a small flock of nuns passed, chatting in bright voices that filled the air like hawthorn petals on the wind. The man on the bicycle went on riding back and forth, looking at us expectantly now and again.

"Is this where we're meeting the man from Scotland Yard as well?" I asked.

"Yes. The fellow on the bicycle," Mr. Scant said matter-of-factly, as though it were so obvious as to go without saying.

"Oh! So, um . . . do we have to wait for Uncle Reggie before we can talk to him?"

"That's the conundrum we find ourselves in."

After that, we fell silent again. I took to watching the boats bumping and scraping their way down the Seine. Still, Uncle Reggie didn't appear. Sensing movement, I turned to see Mr. Scant taking out his pocket watch with an agitated look. "There's no helping it," he said, and marched toward the man on the bicycle. The man pedaled toward us insouciantly.

"It's odd to see a jackdaw—" he began, but Mr. Scant waved a hand in irritation.

"I'm sure there's some pass phrase we're meant to

give you, but we don't know it. My brother Reginald was meant to supply it, but he's not here."

The man on the bicycle frowned. He was an oddly shaped fellow, with a skinny body but the thick, tapering legs of a keen cyclist, and a narrow, pointed face with a rather feeble mustache. "I think you must have made a mistake of some sort, chaps," he said in a clear English accent. "I'm just an ordinary cycle enthusiast, training for tomorrow's Paris-Roubaix. But it's odd to see a jackdaw flying—"

"My good friend took a bullet to secure for your people what I have in this bag. I ask you to consider what your superiors will say if you come back empty-handed because of your wretched jackdaw."

The man eyed the bag for a moment, then adjusted the cap on his head. "I suppose you're right about that. Alright, then. This will mean more paperwork, but I'm sure some *i*'s and *t*'s can go undotted and uncrossed. You are Mr. Scant, I presume."

"You have me at a disadvantage."

"Well, I should hope so," the mustached man said. "But this probably won't be the last time we meet. You may call me Jackdaw."

"Is that really necessary?"

"In Scotland Yard, or at least in my department,

what is necessary comes second to what works."

Mr. Scant nodded, as though finding that sentiment agreeable. "Here are the items. No need to check them."

The man took the little sack and glanced inside anyway. "If I'm honest, I wouldn't have the faintest idea what to check for anyway. But rest assured, this is appreciated by the powers that be. It won't be forgotten."

"Are you going to restore the contents to their owners?"

Mr. Jackdaw thought for a while. "Yes, I think it's safe to say we will return them to where they belong. First, my superiors may believe we can use them to catch more ne'er-do-wells, but after *that*, you have my solemn word that these will be restored to their rightful owners. And as gesture of my thanks—here, have some chocolate bonbons. They're from Belgium."

I took the little paper bag he proffered, tied with a yellow ribbon. Inside were what looked like sugared quail eggs. "Thank you," I said.

"You're welcome," said Mr. Jackdaw. "I got them especially for you, young Master Diplexito. Please give my regards to your father. I hold his engines in very high regard."

"Oh," I said. "I will. And good luck in your race."

"Thank you. Of course, it wouldn't do for me to stand out by *winning* the thing. I shall simply stay with the peloton and enjoy the views, don't you know? This one is a mere warm-up for the Paris–Brest–Paris, in any case." These place names he said in a rather exaggerated French accent, and then sighed happily. "Now *there's* a race. Well then, my thanks once more—and for now, *adieu*."

After giving a little bow from atop his bicycle, the man pedaled away, holding the handlebar with one hand while the other held the bag containing the cigar box.

"You gave him a lot of information he may not have already had," said Mr. Scant.

I looked up at Mr. Scant in surprise. "Me?"

"It can't be helped now."

"When he was talking about his race?"

Mr. Scant only needed to give me a look, and then I realized what he meant.

"When he said my name . . ."

"Next time we're in the ice house, we'll get to work on your poker face. But first, where on Earth is Reggie?"

Uncle Reggie was nowhere to be found. We had chosen a pleasant hotel on the rue des Beaux-Arts, close to Notre Dame, which had large rooms to accommodate the four of us. With Uncle Reggie missing and Dr. Mikolaitis now hospitalized, the hotel seemed unnaturally empty. I tried Uncle Reggie's door, but it was locked, so I knocked softly and called for him. There was no answer.

"It's awfully quiet here," I said.

"A good time to practice your lock-picking."

"Oh," I said, reaching into my breast pocket for the tools. "Two and five this time?"

Mr. Scant nodded, so I set about trying to pick the lock of Uncle Reggie's door. One pick had to go in the top part of the lock and the other at the bottom, which was not as easy as it sounded. When I fumbled with pick number five and dropped it, Mr. Scant let out such an aggrieved sigh I looked at him in surprise.

"Is everything alright?" I asked.

"With haste, if you please, Master Oliver."

That only made it more difficult to concentrate. I tried to feel for the little latches inside the lock, as

Mr. Scant had taught me, but pressing them all down at once proved difficult. The hardest part was getting the barrel to turn once all the parts were pressed down, which took several tries.

"I'm doing my best," I said.

"I appreciate that, Master Oliver," said Mr. Scant, looking away.

Eventually, I got the picks at just the right angle to hold everything down in the right way and twist. The door creaked open.

"Shall we go inside?" I said.

"Master Oliver, you don't have to ask my permission for every little thing."

I nodded and cautiously stepped through the door. It only took a moment to realize that not only was Uncle Reggie not inside, he had vacated the room altogether. Though seemingly allergic to neatness in his day-to-day life, he had left the bed made and the dresser tidy. A sheet of notepaper, blotted and smudged, sat on the dresser. Mr. Scant hurried over to snatch it up.

"What does it say?"

"So typical of him," Mr. Scant muttered, then looked at me. "Reggie sends his apologies, but apparently he couldn't wait for us to do things the way we planned. He says he's worried sick about Elspeth, so has gone off to investigate her school."

"Ah," I said.

Though Mr. Scant's face was calm, the way he crumpled his brother's note in his hand made his feelings clear.

"Did he say when he'll be back?" I asked.

"For dinner, he said."

"Ah. Shall we have some tea, then?"

"Perhaps not a bad idea."

I went to my room to wait while Mr. Scant prepared tea in the little kitchenette. I sat on the corner of my rather modestly sized hotel bed and tried to sort through everything that was happening, but I kept thinking about Dr. Mikolaitis in the hospital. Mr. Scant had told me that whenever I had a free minute, I ought to do my target practice, so tossed my rolled-up travel gloves from bed to drawer a few times, but soon grew tired of that. When Mr. Scant came in with a tray of tea, he found me with my head in my hands.

"It's all a bit too much," I said.

"Master Oliver?"

"Dr. Mikolaitis in the hospital, Mr. Binns's son out to get us . . . now Uncle Reggie going off on his own. Don't you think it's too much?"

"The only one who can decide what is too much is you, Master Oliver. You are master of your thoughts."

"Well, I can see you're worried too."

"Your tea."

Mr. Scant busied himself with his own cup for a moment. All of a sudden, it struck me that even though taking tea together had become common-place for the two of us, for many years he was merely a rather frightening member of Father's staff—a tall, forbidding man I would avoid speaking to unless I had to. Not until I discovered his hidden life, steal-ing artworks from secret societies and restoring them to their rightful owners, did I begin to consider Mr. Scant someone I could relax with over a hot cup of tea. I smiled a little. It was very British, but no matter how violent the maelstrom we found ourselves in, teatime felt like an island of safety.

"Are you angry at Uncle Reggie?" I asked, as Mr. Scant sat down on the chair by the dresser.

"It's very typical of him to go off and get into trouble. His problem is the opposite of yours. He is too impulsive."

"You think I should be more impulsive?"

"Not more impulsive, Master Oliver. More decisive. Initiative is the key. At some stage, the apprentice has to start acting without the master."

I frowned. "So I should stop asking you what to do?"

"As long as you can make the right decisions."

"But how do I know if they're right or not?"

"That's precisely what you must begin thinking about."

I nodded to myself and took a longer sip of my tea. Then I put my cup down onto its saucer with resolve. "In that case, I shall make the next decision. Uncle Reggie's gone off on his own, and we both know he's not one to keep himself out of trouble. So we ought to finish our tea and then go to find him. What do you say to that, Mr. Scant?"

Mr. Scant nodded. "A sound proposition, Master Oliver. *After* we finish our tea."

III

Chocolate Bonbons

Elspeth Gaunt's place of learning, the *École normale supérieure*, had a special branch in Sèvres, in the southwest of Paris, for women so gifted that stuffy old academics had to admit they should receive a university education too. On the way, I imagined a striking but pretty boarding school with a prim little garden that blossomed with spring flowers. Which was why Mr. Scant's description of what we were looking for took me by surprise.

"It's in a factory?" I said.

"Well, yes and no," said Mr. Scant. "The *manufacture nationale de Sèvres*. There are two sites, the old *manufacture* and the new *manufacture*. The school is in the old building. The new one is far larger; we passed it after we crossed the river."

"With the statues?" I recalled the place, which we had seen from the cab. I had assumed it was another of Paris's grand art museums. "It didn't look like a factory."

"Indeed not. The *manufacture* has little in common with the sort of factories your father owns. It is a factory for fine ceramics, often commissioned by royalty. The finest porcelain the world has ever seen is wrought by the artists in the main building."

"That sounds nice, but Father says his designers are artists too."

"There's some merit to that," Mr. Scant said. "I hope one day your father's motorcars will be as beautiful as his dinner services. In any case, Elspeth's school is one of the institutions occupying the old factory building, which is also a handsome sight. Ah, we have a view now."

Quite unlike a pretty little schoolhouse, the exterior of the former *manufacture de Sèvres* was large and imposing but simple, reminding me of Buckingham Palace. It was a long building with dozens of uniform windows. A tasteful central section stood out from the rest. The awning at the top looked a little like the front of a locomotive smashing through the roof. This being late on a Sunday afternoon, the school was closed. A tall iron fence ran the length of the building, and the gate was shut tight. There wasn't a soul to be seen.

Without my noticing, Mr. Scant had slipped on his claw. He walked briskly to the gate and found it locked, but had it open before I even caught up. For a moment, I was hurt that he hadn't asked me to pick the lock, but I appreciated we had to be quick. If someone were spying out at us from one of the windows, numerous as books in a bookcase, my clumsy lock-picking would have been very conspicuous.

Mr. Scant led me through the open gate and to the French windows ahead, but they were closed and there was no doorbell to ring. The school interior was dark. Mr. Scant knocked loudly with his gloved hand, having stashed away the claw as imperceptibly as he had made it appear, but he was met with empty silence.

"There are smaller buildings to try," said Mr. Scant. "It would be better to find some staff than to break in."

"I don't see Uncle Reggie. Do you think he came here, looking for his daughter?"

Mr. Scant didn't answer. We began to make our way around the large building, with Mr. Scant occasionally peering through windows, until we found an attractive pavilion with a carefully tended garden and a grand stone staircase. The stairs led to a small building with a pointed roof. We made our way there, and Mr. Scant cautiously looked all around the area before knocking on the door.

Immediately, he heard a rather loud crash, the first sign of life we had encountered since making our way into the school grounds. There was silence for a moment, as if the person inside were considering whether or not to ignore us, but then came the sound of hurried footsteps, and after a few prolonged seconds, the door opened abruptly. A red-faced man with a thick mustache looked at Mr. Scant with fire in his eyes. The sides of his mustache twitched a little. "*Oui?*" he said.

Mr. Scant began to apologize, in French, for the interruption, but the man waved his hand in irritation.

"You are English." I couldn't tell what had given Mr. Scant away, but then, my own French was barely strong enough to follow the average conversation anyway. "Let's use English then. I studied at Cambridge."

Mr. Scant nodded courteously. "Your English sounds far better than my French. I'm terribly sorry to have disturbed you."

"Yes, well, how did you get through the gates?"

"The gates? They were open," said Mr. Scant, feigning confusion.

"Hmm? That's irregular," said the man, rubbing his mustache.

Just then, a woman's voice came from somewhere inside the building, asking what was happening. *"Qu'est-ce qui se passe, Paul?"*

"Je ne sais pas encore!" called the man, apparently named Paul. Then he looked at me and seemed to decide that if Mr. Scant had a child with him, he could not be a threat. "What is it that you're after?"

"We're searching for a dear relative," said Mr. Scant. "She receives her education here, but some time has passed since she last contacted her family."

The man nodded sympathetically. "No laughing matter."

"Are you by chance a teacher here at the *école*?" asked Mr. Scant.

"Mostly a researcher, but a teacher on occasion. My name is Langevin."

"Forgive me for not introducing myself. My name is Scant. Are you familiar with Elspeth Gaunt?"

"Ah, the Gaunt girl. Yes, I know her."

"Then do you perchance know her current whereabouts?"

The man tugged again at his mustache. "I don't recall seeing her in a year or more. Hold on, I remember Marie took a liking to the girl. One moment, please."

He allowed us into the entrance hall, but his body language made it clear we ought to stay there as he slipped away. Mr. Scant looked down at me and raised his eyebrows, but I wasn't sure why. After a moment, the man returned with a woman who looked as though she aimed to have the appearance of a schoolmarm, only to be thwarted by wild, frizzy hair that had no intention of staying in its bun. She wore a plain smock, and her deep-set eyes flicked between us inquisitively.

Mr. Scant bowed his head. "Madame Curie," he said, and I felt my mouth open involuntarily—the famous lady physicist, as I lived and breathed. "Permit me to introduce myself. I am Elspeth Gaunt's uncle. My name is Scant. You of course need no introduction."

Madame Marie Curie smiled a little and answered in an accent that to my ear sounded a little like Dr. Mikolaitis's, "You flatter me, sir. And who is this dear child?"

"My apprentice, Master Diplexito."

"What an interesting name. Now, you say you are Elspeth's uncle? She spoke often of her father but never of you."

"Alas, I did not have a great part in her childhood. But I care dearly for my brother, and he is most anxious to find his daughter. We were hoping to find him here, which would have made matters easier."

"I see. I wish I could help more," Madame Curie said, "but Miss Gaunt concluded her studies almost a year ago, and I haven't seen her since. I should probably tell you that at the time she finished, she wasn't studying here in Sèvres. She was one of a select group of girls studying at the main branch on the . . . How would you say it? Ulm Road? The *rue d'Ulm*. Perhaps you could ask there."

"We'll do that. Please accept our apologies for disturbing you, and thank you for your help, Madame Curie. Monsieur Langevin."

"It was no trouble," said Madame Curie.

"It *was* trouble, but I wish you well," said Monsieur Langevin.

Mr. Scant doffed his hat, and we stepped back outside. I realized that if I didn't speak now, I would in all likelihood never get the chance again, so blurted out, "I hope they give you another Nobel Prize soon, Madame Curie!"

She laughed. "A second Nobel Prize? Wouldn't that be something, Paul?"

Monsieur Langevin gave a little smile that made his mustache go lopsided and nodded to me briefly before closing the door. I looked up at Mr. Scant. "So is the other part of the school nearby?"

"Regretfully, no. We'll need to go back to the city center. But I'm still worried about Reginald. I was rather hoping to see him here. Hopefully we'll rendezvous back at the hotel."

"*Rendez-vous*," I repeated, with my best guttural French *R*, but Mr. Scant ignored me.

Mr. Scant was in no mood for conversation. When I expressed my excitement at having met a famous scientist, he nodded but made no reply. Once he had asked the coachman to take us to the 5th arrondissement, the rest of our journey back toward the city center passed in silence. Mr. Scant was deep in thought, and I didn't want to disturb him, so contented myself with looking out of the window and trying to read the French signage. I had been learning French for two years in school, and while I was by no means the worst in my class, my level of understanding was still poor, and I was grateful Madame Curie had spoken to us in English. When our carriage slowed down to navigate a busy crossroads, I heard a newspaper boy shouting in French, and I was pleased that I could understand the headline. A new aeroplane had taken to the skies—with fourteen people aboard.

After we passed the opulent gardens of Luxembourg Palace, Mr. Scant began to gather his things— we were almost at our destination. We stepped off the coach near the Panthéon, which was busier than Notre Dame had been earlier in the day. The very moment my feet touched the street, I felt a tug at my jacket and looked around to see a young urchin of about nine years old. I almost smiled at how perfectly like the illustrations of street gamins from popular novels he was, with a shapeless cap doing nothing to contain his mass of straggly, sand-colored hair, his clothes a mess of torn material over a shirt several sizes too large for him.

"This way," said Mr. Scant, stalking away from the Panthéon. I made to follow him, but the little urchin did not let go of my jacket. I tried to pull away, but he stared blankly at me with big, green eyes. His nose was running, and I worried what those grubby fingers of his had touched.

"*Est-ce qu'il y a . . . quelque chose?*" I said, trying to ask what he wanted. The boy cocked his head a little, probably at my bad French or worse accent, but his expression didn't change. However, after a moment, he lifted his other palm to me. He was a beggar, probably the most forward beggar I had ever encountered. "Ah," I said, flustered. "*Je . . . Je n'ai pas le . . . l'argent.*"—I don't have any money. "*Mais . . . Ah! Bonbon! Chocolat!*"

I had remembered the little chocolate eggs the man from Scotland Yard had given me, which I still had in my pocket. They were a little warm, but the boy's face lit up like the sun when I put them into his outstretched palm. His eyes had already been like saucers, but they seemed to grow dangerously large and then began to water as he thanked me over and over before scurrying away. He grinned back at me just for a moment before disappearing behind Mr. Rodin's famous statue of *The Thinker*.

Mr. Scant hadn't waited to see if I had followed him. Fortunately, given his height, he was not difficult to spot, so I ran to catch up. The *École normale supérieure*, where Elspeth had studied, was a short walk away. Its gates were open, and even at this time on a Sunday evening, plenty of people milled about the entrance: a large doorway flanked by little columns supporting two handsome statues of seated scholarly women. As we passed through the gates, Mr. Scant blinked in surprise as he heard someone call out his name in a French accent. A rather dapper young man with a round face and straggly beard was running toward us. "You are Mr. Scant?"

"I am he," said Mr. Scant.

"You're just as your brother described. He wanted me to give you this."

The young stranger handed over a piece of paper, folded haphazardly. *Heck*, Uncle Reggie's nickname for his brother, was scrawled on the top, with a large blot of ink.

"Ah. I am indebted to you," said Mr. Scant. "How did you know who to look for?"

"An Englishman with a face like an eagle, with a boy like a barn owl, he said!" the young man replied with relish.

"I see."

"He also said you would be happy to reimburse me for my inconvenience," said the cheerful young man. "I said I was happy to help a brother who supports the Cause."

"Ah, the Cause," said Mr. Scant. "We must do our best for the Cause."

"With all my heart!" said the earnest young man. I was certain Mr. Scant had no more idea what the Cause was than I did, but Uncle Reggie had a gift for convincing people he was on their side.

"Why didn't Uncle Reggie leave a note for us at the other school, where we met Madame Curie?" I asked Mr. Scant.

"Perhaps he knew to come here directly but didn't see fit to share the information," said Mr. Scant. He began to open the letter, but the young man was still standing expectantly. Mr. Scant paused, then with only a very slight pursing of his lips, pulled out a few coins and gave them to the young man. "For the Cause," he said.

"For the Cause," the young man answered, and walked away satisfied, tossing his francs in the air and catching them.

"What did Uncle Reggie say?" I asked, as Mr. Scant read the note, a frown on his face.

"He says the records show Elspeth graduated over a year ago and hasn't been seen since. But apparently a young man Reggie describes as, I quote, 'a little toff,' told him he'd better stay away from a private gallery not far from here. So he's gone to investigate."

"What should we do?"

"What do you think we should do, Master Oliver?"

"Oh yes," I said, remembering Mr. Scant wanted me to take the initiative. I thought for a moment. "Honestly, I think Uncle Reggie is getting himself into trouble again. And if someone took him aside, it sounds as though we're expected here, so we may well be walking into a trap. If we follow Uncle Reggie to the gallery, we'll probably be playing into their hands as well. But on the other hand, our only alternative is to leave and hope Uncle Reggie is alright. I'd rather go and make sure, so we'll have to go carefully."

Mr. Scant nodded. "Good. You're beginning to think well. The gallery is this way."

It was less than ten minutes' walk. We first made a circuit of the private gallery, which was a large building that had probably started life as a rich person's townhouse and had a sort of courtyard garden of its own. But high walls surrounded it, and the iron gates of the gallery entrance had been closed and chained.

"No sign of Uncle Reggie," I said. Mr. Scant grunted.

We gained entry to the premises the simplest way we could: we found the quietest part of the periphery, where Mr. Scant let me step up onto his hands so that I could reach the top of the wall and then pull him up. As soon as I could see over the wall, though, I dropped back down. Mr. Scant caught and steadied me awkwardly.

"What is it?" he said.

"There are men at the door with guns," I replied.

"Did they see you?"

"I don't think so. But one of them was really big. The men, I mean, not the gun. Actually, the gun w—"

I didn't get any further than that, because Mr. Scant held up a hand to stop me, as if he had heard something strange.

"What is it?" I said, after a pause.

"We were followed," he growled, and before I could so much as register what he had said, he took off toward the nearest corner like a dog after a pigeon.

I sighed and brushed myself off before running after him. As I approached the corner, I saw Mr. Scant had stopped immediately after rounding it.

He was looming over the small street child from earlier that day, the one to whom I had bequeathed my chocolate eggs from Mr. Jackdaw. In fact, some of that chocolate was still visible across the boy's face—smeared across his cheeks, presumably during an attempt to clean himself up. A tear was crossing the smudge now, as the boy blinked up at the gargoyle looming over him.

"It's you!" I said, mostly to encourage Mr. Scant to put his fangs away. When the boy saw me, his terrified face crumpled. He let out a cry that I doubted would have made any more sense if I were fluent in French, and buried his face in my chest. I cringed as I imagined what was being wiped onto my shirt, but as he began to bawl, I patted him comfortingly on the cleanest patch of his hat.

Once the boy had calmed down enough to speak coherently, I knelt down until I was below his eye level, something that my schoolmate Chudley had taught me was good for calming down his little sister. Mr. Scant looked as though he wanted to stalk away, but I needed him to translate the boy's French, so I beckoned him over. Mr. Scant listened with a disdainful look on his face as the boy spoke. I could identify a word here and there but not the sense of what he was saying. Still, I could understand that the boy kept repeating a name—Julien.

After a time, Mr. Scant stood up. From the fact that he had listened so long to a little orphan boy without interruption, I knew that the boy must have mentioned something of interest. "What did he say?" I asked.

"He said, and I shall have to take some liberties with translation, that some unsavory gentlemen have taken his brother away and locked him in the gallery we were investigating. He thought you must be a very kind person because you gave him chocolates, so he was sure you were searching for his brother and the others who have been taken away. And he knows a good place to get over the wall."

"Do you think this has anything to do with Miss Gaunt?"

"That I can't say. Do you think we ought to investigate, Master Oliver?"

"Yes," I said. "Yes, I do."

And so it was that we found ourselves behind a gazebo in the courtyard of an art gallery, peering around a corner at two men with a big Hotchkiss gun. The place the boy had led us to did not, strictly speaking, provide easy entry into the gallery, but we at least seized the possibility. Two of the outer walls were lower at the corner where they met, and on the other side stood the gazebo, behind which we could hide. Mr. Scant had boosted me up again, and with all my strength, I had pulled him up after me. Once he had reached the top of the wall, he reached back for the little French boy, then dropped down on the other side to help us both down silently. And now Mr. Scant had run out to face the men with the big Hotchkiss.

When the great bark of gunfire sounded, the little boy jolted forward to see what had happened, but I held him back. When all was quiet, I peered around the gazebo again to see Mr. Scant propping the two unconscious men against the wall. He positioned them so that they leaned against one another, then fastidiously began to tie their legs together.

"Nasty business," he said, loudly enough for me to hear, a clear signal that the coast was clear. "Thugs like these know what they've signed up for, so I don't feel too much guilt about heavy blows to the head. We must hope I didn't do them any lasting damage."

The boy followed me out into the open and stood gaping at the Hotchkiss gun. I knocked his hand away when he reached out to touch it, before going to the doors to see if the lock needed picking. When I tried the handles, the gallery doors swung open with ease. I glanced around, but the hallway inside was empty. "The door's open," I said. "Are we ready to go in?"

"If you're ready, then I am too."

"What about the boy?"

Mr. Scant regarded the boy as though a rather ragged kitten had taken to following us. "He's safer with us than here."

"Come on," I said to the child, holding out my hand and trying to remember the way to say it in French. "Erm . . . *on y va?*" I chanced, and whether it was the right thing to say or he was just going by my gesture, the boy hurried over and took my hand. He had a surprisingly tight grip.

Inside the private gallery, all was quiet. The rooms looked as though they hadn't been used for a long time. Some paintings hung on the walls, and some sculptures and fine vases were displayed here and there, but mostly the gallery was full of large boxes and crates, standing empty. In one room, we found a suspicious curtain, but behind it was nothing but a canvas on which an artist had painted Napoleon III—well enough to be recognizable but badly enough that he also looked a bit like Mrs. Prigg, the wife of our games master at school. We found nothing more until the boy tugged on my arm and pointed to a door set in the side of a staircase. I thought it would be a storage cupboard, but when Mr. Scant opened it, another staircase was revealed, obviously not meant for the public. It led down into a basement of some sort.

The boy began to hug my arm as we descended. Mr. Scant struck a match once inside the dark stairwell, and I found two dirty old oil lamps on top of another crate. Mr. Scant lit them both, leaving one where it was and taking the other with him.

My foot slipped a little, and I realized there was something wet on the floor, dark and a little viscous. I wasn't certain, but it looked like blood. Feeling strangely comforted by the little street urchin's grip, I stepped closer to Mr. Scant.

He had seen the blood too, and lowered the lamp for a closer look. There was a clear trail, almost as though some monstrous snail had made its way across the floor, but rather more like someone had dragged someone bleeding into another large crate up against the far wall.

We pressed closer to the crate until we could see its official-looking letters stamped on the side. They read, *To Shanghai.*

"Hold this," said Mr. Scant, passing the lamp to me. He used his claw to work around the edges of the crate's nearest side, and pulled once or twice, but had to detach the longest of claw's blades and use it in the manner of a crowbar to pry the thing open. The whole of one side fell to the floor with a crash, sending up a cloud of dust. The little boy let out a yelp of surprise, but whether because of the sound or the sight within, I could not tell.

Uncle Reggie was a terrible sight, bloody-faced and motionless in the darkness.

IV

Buckets and Baguettes

r. Scant's lips were pressed into a straight line as he knelt by his brother and listened for breathing.

"He's alive," Mr. Scant said. "Well, after all, there would be no sense in shipping a dead body to China."

"They put food and water in there with him too," I said, holding the lamp up to the small baguettes and apples by Uncle Reggie's feet. There were also a number of uncorked wine bottles and a large bucket with a lid. Whoever put him inside clearly intended to stave off Uncle Reggie's starvation—which also meant that the person, or persons, intended for Reggie to stay trapped for a considerable length of time. "Is he hurt badly?"

"He's been given a good thrashing, that's for sure. What is that child doing?"

The boy's voice rang out clear as a bell, over and over. He was going to all the other crates in the room and knocking on them, calling out, "Julien?"

"He's looking for his brother," I said. "He must have disappeared like Uncle Reggie did." Then I went over to the boy and shushed him. "*Les hommes . . . dangereux*," I said, which I was fairly sure meant *dangerous men*.

But the boy wasn't swayed. A stream of impassioned French flowed from his lips, and while I could guess he was talking about his missing brother, I couldn't understand a word. The little boy turned instead to Mr. Scant. For his part, Mr. Scant listened, took another brief look at his brother, then went to the boy and hoisted him up onto the top of the open crate. From this vantage point, the boy could see the tops of all of the other crates, and his grubby face fell. Like the boy, I wasn't tall enough to see, but I understood what his expression meant. None of the other crates had lids on. They were all open, because they were empty.

"*Comprends-tu?*" said Mr. Scant, and the boy nodded. He understood. His brother was not here. Nevertheless, he continued to search the room in case there was something else to find, this time without the calls for his brother.

Mr. Scant stomped on a plank of wood until it split, then used it as a makeshift splint for Uncle Reggie's arm. The bone must have been broken. "Help me a moment," he said, then set about getting his brother upright. I helped as carefully as I could, putting my hands where Mr. Scant's were and heaving Uncle Reggie upright. Reggie was completely unconscious, so this was no easy task. Unbidden, I remembered how Mr. Scant often spoke about the dangers of knocking a man unconscious, how it often caused injuries that lasted a lifetime. It was small comfort to remember Dr. Mikolaitis's grim smile as he had said, "True enough, but remember, even among pugilists knocked out for the count dozens of times, one or two of them can still remember how to spell their names."

As we made our way to the stairs, the boy ran out in front of us with his fists clenched. "*Mais Julien . . .*"

"*Julien n'est pas ici,*" growled Mr. Scant. "*Désolé.*" Julien is not here. I'm sorry.

The boy's lip trembled, but he turned away from us for one more circuit around the empty basement. Getting Uncle Reggie up the stairs was another ordeal, but we managed, mostly by Mr.

Scant positing himself under his brother's unbroken arm and half-lifting, half-dragging him. Once at the top of the stairs, it became easier to support him in a more dignified manner. Mr. Scant turned to me. "Go out and call a cab. Bring it here. We'll have to pretend he's drunk."

I didn't question the plan, only rushed to put it into motion. I was already passing through the doors when I realized the little boy was running alongside me. Thinking he would probably fare better with me than with Mr. Scant, I said nothing. Outside the doors lay the two guards, who were still down for the count. Looking back at them nervously a few times, I picked the lock on the iron gates so quickly I surprised myself. I glanced at the boy to see if he was impressed, but he seemed to think nothing of my feat.

Outside the gallery, the road was quiet, and I didn't know which way I ought to go.

"Where can we get a hackney?" I asked the boy. "A cab? Car? Carriage?"

The boy scratched his nose in an endearing but unhelpful show of confusion.

"You know, a hackney cab? A growler?" I mimed a driver cracking his whip and then the horse rearing, which was perhaps a bit elaborate but seemed to work, because the boy's face lit up. He said something in French, took my hand, and led me off down the road.

Two corners later, we came to a road large enough for a number of cabs and motorcars to be making their way up and down it. I waved at one driver, who slowed his carriage but then noticed the boy standing with me and drove away again, pointedly sticking his nose up in the air. The boy pulled his cap over his face in shame. Annoyed, I took his hand and stepped forward with him as I waved down the next driver, who stopped and eyed us suspiciously.

"*Musée de . . .* " I began, trying in vain to recall the name of the gallery where we had found Uncle Reggie. I looked to the boy. "*Quoi?*"

"Ah!" The boy named the gallery—*Musée Holland*, I thought I heard—to the driver. The boy then explained in French that two men were waiting for us there. I couldn't have repeated what he said in his little chirruping voice but could at least follow the meaning. The coachman seemed to accept that the little ragamuffin was acting as an interpreter on my behalf, probably for a few centimes, so he nodded and gestured for us to get in.

We rode the cab the short distance to the gallery, me sitting inside while the boy simply clung to the exterior. When Mr. Scant and Uncle Reggie came into view, Mr. Scant had draped his coat over Uncle Reggie's broken arm and was moving him in such a way that Uncle Reggie appeared to be swaying like a drunkard. Mr. Scant had also strategically placed one of the crate's wine bottles just behind them, which struck me as a clever touch.

After Mr. Scant heaved Uncle Reggie into the cab, I settled him into the seat, propping him against the side of the carriage so he wouldn't slip down. I heard an angry yelp, and to my surprise saw Mr. Scant deposit the little boy into the carriage with us. The boy was objecting, gesturing to the gallery and saying something about his brother Julien again, but Mr. Scant said something low and menacing to him. I was once again amazed by how wide the boy's eyes could open when he was shocked. A moment later, the child scrambled to the window to look at the road ahead of us.

"What did you tell him?" I asked Mr. Scant.

"The truth," Mr. Scant answered. "That we are being watched, and that the moment we leave him alone, he will be snatched up just like his brother was."

"We're being followed?" I repeated, peering out of the window, but Mr. Scant was speaking to the driver and we were in motion. Standing in the road was a solitary figure in a wide-brimmed traveler's hat and a long black coat that appeared very expensive and well-tailored. It hung down almost to the man's shoes, a pair of well-shined oxfords that were the only clear indication whether this figure was male or female. "Do we need to fight?"

"Not if we can avoid it, with Reggie injured and the child here."

The carriage rolled on, conveying us toward the figure. The man lifted his head as we passed him, so I met his eye. He was young, with his dark hair worn long and his eyebrows thick and angry-looking, but that was all I could perceive as he pulled up his scarf. As he adjusted it, I noticed he wore a ring set with a gemstone, the blue of lapis lazuli, not so large as to be vulgar but noticeable even in such a brief moment. The man continued to hold my gaze as we passed, until the carriage left him behind and we turned a corner.

Realizing I had been holding my breath all the while, I exhaled.

The girl at the hotel reception looked as though she had heard the last trumpet for Judgment Day when she saw us bring in Uncle Reggie and the unkempt street boy. She gaped at us but said nothing as we tipped our hats and made our way to our rooms.

As we eased Uncle Reggie down onto his bed, I let out a sigh. "First Dr. Mikolaitis, now Uncle Reggie . . ."

"Our allies are dwindling," said Mr. Scant.

"We have a new one, though." I looked at the boy and felt embarrassed that I didn't know his name. But that was one thing I knew how to ask in French. *"Comment t'appelles-tu?"*

"Victor," said the boy, in a small voice.

"J'espère que . . . tu trouveras ton frère," I said, hoping that meant I hoped he would find his brother. I could never remember how the future tense worked in French.

"*'Ci,*" Victor said, looking away.

Mr. Scant had gone to fill a bucket with warm water before cleaning his brother's wounds. The bruises on Uncle Reggie's face looked raw and painful, darkening the crow's-feet around his eyes into strange black veins.

"Do you need help?" I said.

"I don't think there is much you can do, Master Oliver," said Mr. Scant. "You ought to rest."

"I don't feel like resting."

"Then perhaps some quiet time."

Mr. Scant hadn't looked at me since he came in. He was wringing out the washcloth and delicately applying it to his brother's face. I didn't want to irritate him. "I know, I'll take Victor to have a bath."

"Probably a good idea, for all our sakes," Mr. Scant said absently.

"Can I give him some of my clothes? The ones he's wearing are all torn and they're too big for him anyway. Mine will probably fit at least as well."

"Master Oliver, I am merely your father's valet. It is not my place to tell you to whom you may and may not give your belongings. Though I would caution that your mother would sorely miss any of your Sunday clothes, were you to make gifts of them."

I nodded and led Victor away to my room. His stomach rumbled as we walked, so I gave him a lump of sugar from the sugar pot. That seemed to lift his spirits.

At home, one of the maids, Meg or Penny, would always run the bath for me. So I enjoyed watching as Paris's famous modern water systems slowly filled our hotel bathtub. The water let off a welcoming steam. I added some chamomile and put the soap and eau de toilette on the flattest part of the bathtub. "Goodbye, washcloth," I said, putting that alongside them.

When the tub was full, I turned to Victor and gestured toward the bath before stepping out of the bathroom. While Victor was bathing, I could pick out clothes he could wear. I thought I ought to send a telegram to Dr. Mikolaitis and tell him what had happened too.

A moment later, the bathroom door opened and Victor appeared, looking perplexed.

"What is it?" I said, then remembered myself and asked it again in French.

I wasn't sure about Victor's reply, but I thought he asked why I closed the door on him.

"You can have a bath," I said. "Bath time. Erm . . . *baignes? Tu baignes?*"

Victor laughed and went to sit by the dresser.

"Come on, now, you need a bath," I said.

"No, please, thank you," he replied.

I stopped. "You can speak English?"

"English," said Victor. "Yes, no, plis, senk you, 'allo, g'bye. English!"

"I . . . Well, that's a good start," I said. "Now, bath."

"Bath."

"Let's go. Bath."

I led him to the bathroom again and pointed to the hot, welcoming water.

"Master Olivier," said Victor.

"*Oliver*," I said. "Not 'Olivier.' Oliver."

"Olivia?"

"Oliver."

"Master Olivia!" Victor looked very proud of himself.

"You can call me Ollie." I pointed to my face. "*Ollie*."

"Ollie!"

Sorting that out didn't get us any closer to making him bathe. The more I gestured to the bath, the more he shook his head and laughed.

"How do I put this? You're a bit . . . noisome. Malodorous?" When there was no light of comprehension in the boy's eyes, I had to resort to a very obvious gesture. Waving a hand in front of my nose, I intoned, "I'm afraid you really smell bad."

I had been so concerned with getting the boy to understand that I hadn't considered his feelings. His little face fell and he hung his head. Then he swallowed and mumbled, "*D'accord*." I understand.

I left him in private to get into the bath, busying myself with the telegram to Dr. Mikolaitis. I considered sending one to Father, but thought it would be better to get Mr. Scant's opinion first.

Once I had sorted out the clothes I would be the least upset about losing, I thought I had better check on the boy. He wasn't used to baths, and I was a little worried he would drown, so I knocked on the door and took the pile of clothes inside.

There was a little set of metal shelves on which I could put the clothes, but as I did so, I saw Victor and frowned. He was sitting in the bath, but his face and hair were entirely dry, still caked in dirt.

"What are you doing?" I said. "Why aren't you washing your face?" I mimed splashing my face with water. Victor, who had obviously been expecting this moment, rattled off a stream of French I couldn't follow at all. His arms, different colors above and below where they'd soaked in the water, made a series of gestures, ending with him holding out the washcloth and soap to me expectantly.

"You can wash yourself," I said. "You're old enough. Well, Meg and Penny probably helped me at your age, but they aren't here, so this is a good chance for you to learn."

Victor responded in English. "No no no no."

"You do it," I said firmly.

Victor looked crestfallen and flopped over the edge of the bath, letting washcloth and soap slip from his hands. "How can someone with nobody to spoil him be so spoilt?" I said.

Grateful Victor couldn't understand that, I went over to pick up the things he'd dropped. The various scented soaps and lotions I had added to the bath had formed a thick foam that protected Victor's modesty, which was good, because from what I gathered from playground rhymes, the French were markedly less concerned about such matters. For my own part, I was English to the core and a happy member of the large majority of boys who would never shower at school, even after games, and would wait until I got home. That, in my opinion, was simply the English way.

But Victor was not English, and rather than take the washcloth when proffered, he gave an eager nod and turned his back expectantly. "Oh, very well," I murmured, dipped the cloth into the filthy water, and began to wash the grime from the little boy's back.

He chirruped at me in French as I scrubbed. Getting the boy's skin clean became something of a game to me, and as washcloth and foam alike became progressively murkier, the pinkish hue of the boy's skin was revealed. I scrubbed at his face and neck as he shut his eyes tight. He refused to put his head under the water, so I used the small tin bucket left in the bathroom for the purpose of wetting his hair.

As the water straightened Victor's tangle of locks, it became clear how long his hair really was. If not for it floating in the browny-gray water, the strands would have been long enough to hang halfway down his back. I rubbed the bar of soap in my hands until I got a lather and then used that to run through the boy's hair, though there was no taming the tangles without a comb.

"The rest you can do yourself," I said, to which the boy nodded as if he understood, though I wasn't sure that was the case. Still, he made no objections as I withdrew, singing happily to himself. Wrinkling my nose a little, I picked up his pile of rags as I departed, and when I was back in the main room, I threw it all into the little corner hearth. It wasn't lit, but we could watch the pile go up in flames when we made a fire this evening.

Still not wanting to stray too far from Victor, I decided I would have to make myself some tea. The problem was I had no idea where Mr. Scant procured the boiling water. As I searched, I heard a loud cry from the bathroom and then the door slamming against the wall. For a moment, I feared Victor had come running out of the bath with no clothes on, but he had at least pulled on my old black shorts, which almost reached his knees. He cast about the room with his big, round eyes.

"What is it? Er . . . *qu'est-ce que . . . ?*" I began, but the boy pointed at the fireplace and gave a yelp of outrage before running over to dig through the pile of rags.

"Those are dirty!" I said. "If it's your hat, that's still on the stand outside. I haven't—"

That was as far as I could get before Victor pulled out the undershirt he had been wearing. While less ragged than his jacket or trousers, it was still much too large for him and in no fit state to wear.

"I gave you a shirt," I said. "It's in there with the rest."

The roar of bullets from the Hotchkiss gun that we'd heard earlier paled beside the sudden deluge of angry French that came from Victor's mouth. He held up the shirt angrily, then gestured at the fireplace, hopping up and down in outrage, his wet feet slapping against the floorboards. I caught the occasional word here and there, especially *Julien*, from which I surmised the shirt was precious to him because it had been given to him by his brother.

"Julien?" I said. "Julien's shirt? Alright. Alright. *Je comprends. Désolé.* Alright! Just dry your hair. Your hair! With the towel! No, you can do it. You can do it alone! Fine. Fine. I'll help."

As I wrapped the boy's head in the towel and set about trying to get it all dry, I wondered aloud how he had ever managed to fend for himself. I supposed there were others out there on the streets who would look after him in their fashion, like in Mr. Dickens's story that Mother loved so much. Giving the filthy shirt a liberal dose of scented water and helping Victor into my waistcoat and jacket, I was impressed by how he had transformed. He resembled a slightly ferocious cherub.

Eager to show off the transformation, I went to show Mr. Scant. "Mr. Scant, look how neat Victor looks now!" I said. "He refused to change his shirt, though, so sorry if it . . ."

My voice trailed off, because Mr. Scant had turned to us with a finger to his lips. I realized that he was holding a small bottle of smelling salts under his brother's nose. Uncle Reggie was looking at us blearily. He was awake.

"What's all this then?" he croaked. "Oliver, my lad, and who's this other fellow? There is another one, isn't there? I'm not seeing things?"

"This is Victor," I said. "He helped us find you."

"Victor!" said Victor. "Victor, Ollie."

Uncle Reggie gave a little smile. "How is it I don't get to call you Ollie but he does?"

"Because he says 'Oliver' like 'Olivia'!"

"Olivier!" Victor said helpfully.

Uncle Reggie started to laugh but then winced in pain and quickly settled down. "Ow. Ow. Ouchy bloody hell," he rumbled, which I pretended not to hear.

"Try not to get excited," said Mr. Scant. "Three of your ribs are broken."

"Only three?" his brother asked.

"Three *ribs*. The rest of your body's a good deal worse off."

"They did me in good and proper, didn't they?"

"So it would seem," Mr. Scant said. "Now that everybody's here, why not tell us what happened?"

I sat down on the chair that matched the hotel's dressing table, and Victor sat at my feet. After thinking to himself for a little while, Uncle Reggie began: "Well, I suppose I should really start by saying I'm sorry I went off on my own, although as I'm sure Heck will remind us all, I'm a pigheaded sort and would do the same thing again even if I knew how it would turn out. Couldn't abide the idea of faffing about in some museum, going after some ne'er-do-well, when I could be out looking for Ellie. I could just imagine, you know, 'Oh, you just missed her, she was here an hour ago but then she got shoved into a carriage with a bag over her head.' Do you see what I mean?"

"You should have told us," said Mr. Scant.

"Well, I didn't, and I don't suppose you'd have changed your plans if I did. I left a note, though, didn't I? I went to that big fancy *école* they sent poor Ellie to and asked around for her."

"How did you know she wasn't at the girls' school?" I asked.

Uncle Reggie blinked at me. "There was a girls' school? What, in a different place?"

"Completely different," I said.

"Well, I didn't know about that. I just went to the big school, and people remembered her there, so I knew it was the right place. I asked around, and this young fellow said he knew her. Well-bred sort, bit la-di-da, fox hunting on Papa's estate, you know? I mean, there's rich like your father rich, Ollie, *industrial* rich, and then there's *old money* rich. You see my meaning? His valet probably has a valet. Ah, my neck is killing me . . ."

"Perhaps we should move on to the point of all this?" Mr. Scant said.

"Alright, so, this toffee-nosed youngster, he's a nasty piece of work. Not nice. You can tell just from how he talks. He says Ellie's meant for better things than I could ever understand and I ought to stay out of her life, only he says it in a way that he can smile and sound charming, like I'm fortunate to even hear him talking. I say I just want to write her a letter, and he says if she wanted to contact me, she'd let me know."

"Who was he?" I asked.

"I can't say for sure. But he adds, very casual, that I ought to stay away from this gallery over by the house where Descartes used to live, and off he sweeps. Exit stage left. So I ask around about where this gallery is, and it's not so far away. And then I ask a student who's sort of loafing around to pass on a message to you, and I go to have a butcher's, as they say in London. And when I found the gallery, no sooner was I at the gates than a couple of great, I don't know, Greco-Roman wrestlers, they looked like . . . they grabbed me and dragged me goodness knows where and flung me down some stairs."

"Father will make sure you get the best doctors money can buy," I said.

"As long as they have some good painkillers, that's all I ask. Your Dr. Mickey Mikolaitis will do me just fine. Where is he, anyway?"

"He was shot," said Mr. Scant. "But we'll talk about that later."

"Shot?"

"By the ne'er-do-well."

"He's only injured," I interjected, feeling that was important information.

"Oh," Uncle Reggie said. "Well, not as though I could have stopped it, really, was it? Was it?"

"You most likely wouldn't have made any differ-ence, no," said his brother. "And now he's probably in a better state than you are, so worry about yourself for now."

"He's in a hospital," I said. "We should probably take you there too."

"Before we proceed, was that all that happened?" said Mr. Scant. "They threw you downstairs and beat you up?"

"Oh, no, no, I was getting to the important part," said Uncle Reggie. "After they roughed me up a bit, the posh boy from the university showed up again."

"Did he have black hair, worn long, and a long coat?"

"Well, I don't know about the coat, but yes, long-haired like a girl, that's the one. One of those little half-wits who fancies himself a Romantic poet. If he didn't have those meatheads, I'd have given him what for. Ow!"

"Don't get yourself worked up. You're in a very poor state," Mr. Scant said, easing his brother back down onto the bed. "You said he was English. Did he say anything to you?"

"Yes," said Uncle Reggie. "Yes, he did. Just before the big fella knocked my lights out, the brat looks down at me with this sneer all across his lips, and he says, 'If you want to see your daughter so much, why don't you join her in China?' That's what he said, 'In China.'" Uncle Reggie looked at his brother with his eyes wide, just now processing the implications of his words. "I think Ellie's in China."

V

The Ferry and Afterward

I had no doubt that we were the subject of much gossip on the ferry-ride home.

We must have looked a peculiar bunch, and no denying it. Tall, brooding Mr. Scant was on his guard, glowering at everyone he suspected might have been a foe. Then there was me, trying to smile apologetically at the sunburnt holidaymakers and well-fed gourmets who had just come face to face with one of Mr. Scant's patented scowls.

And behind us were the two invalids, who the crew had provided with wooden recliners. The two of them had been positioned on the deck in a V-shaped fashion, so that their heads came together. Dr. Mikolaitis was smoking a cigarette while Uncle Reggie fanned himself, which also served to keep the tobacco smoke from blowing in his face. The day was much hotter than average for late March, and Uncle Reggie kept complaining he was boiling in the heat, while Dr. Mikolaitis had procured a straw boater from somewhere or other. He wore the hat low over his eyes, so nothing of his face could be seen.

"Don't fall asleep and burn yourself with your cigarette," I said.

"I don't think I could get much hotter even set alight," grumbled Dr. Mikolaitis.

"Stop your complaining," said Uncle Reggie. "Count yourself lucky. You only hurt in one place. I hurt all over."

"You, sir, were dealt a few blows and received a few bruises," Dr. Mikolaitis said. "I had a piece of metal pierce the full way through my body. The one who should count his lucky stars is you."

"Don't start squabbling again," growled Mr. Scant.

"We're not squabbling!" said Dr. Mikolaitis and Uncle Reggie in unison. I would have laughed, but it was true that their grumbling had gone too far by now. They had been bickering about whose injuries were worse since we retrieved Dr. Mikolaitis from the hospital. Of course, I didn't complain, because

after all, both of them had indeed been hurt griev-
ously. Instead, I sighed.

"You were both so good at being stoic until you
decided this had to be a competition," I said. That
seemed to give them pause. Dr. Mikolaitis put his hat
back over his eyes, and Uncle Reggie redoubled his
fanning efforts.

By then, the ferry had embarked, and we were on
our way back to Britain. I looked back at the land we
had just departed, the land of Voltaire and baguettes
and guillotines. "I hope Victor will be okay," I said
aloud.

The boy had been subdued when we said our
good-byes at the Panthéon. I had written him a letter of introduction that he could deliver to one of
Father's business associates in France, asking the man
to find Victor a good place with people who would
care for him, and I supplied him with more than
enough francs to pay for the journey to the man's
office as well. I would have liked to have taken the
boy myself, and he had cried so much when we told
him we were leaving, but Mr. Scant said that France
was Victor's home and we could always write to his
new patron if we found out anything about Julien.
When the time came to part, as we checked out of

the hotel, there was nothing written on the boy's face but staunch determination.

"I hope the letter I left him with helps him find a new family," I continued, "and that his brother comes back too."

Nobody made any response, so I looked back to Uncle Reggie. We had left the country hoping to find his daughter and bring her home safely. Now we were returning with two invalids, no Elspeth, and only some vague mention of China.

"What are we going to do next?" I asked.

"Why don't you take this and fan me for a bit? That sounds like a good plan," Uncle Reggie said, foisting his paper fan on me.

"I mean about Elspeth," I said, grudgingly taking the fan and flapping it at him. If he had looked smug for a moment about being pampered, that thought sobered him again.

"I suppose I'll have to go to China," he mumbled.

"You're in no state to go to China," said Mr. Scant. "Nor will you be for a good long time."

"I'm just a bit bruised. I'll manage."

"You have six broken bones," Mr. Scant pointed out. "If anyone is going to China, it's me."

"I'll go too," I said.

"You will do no such thing," said Mr. Scant. "This isn't a game, and you have your schoolwork."

"It wasn't a game when Mr. Binns was shooting at us, either!" I protested. "And where would I learn more than on a trip around the world? I already learned so much in Paris."

"I will go alone," said Mr. Scant.

"I'm supposed to be your apprentice," I said.

Mr. Scant didn't answer. Uncle Reggie took the fan back, apparently not satisfied with my efforts, and resumed cooling himself. "No point arguing with him when he's like that, lad," he said. "Heck's as stubborn as stubborn gets."

"I can be stubborn too," I replied. "You wanted me to be able to make my own decisions," I said to Mr. Scant, and even when he raised one eyebrow as if it were a particularly hairy moth taking flight, I was not cowed. "Well, whatever chance you would have in China, you'd have a better chance with me."

"Master Oliver," Mr. Scant said flatly. "There is no question of me taking you to the other side of the world to contend with an unknown threat. We have very little information, and I intend to make use of what little favor we curried with Scotland Yard to gather all the leads I can about Elspeth's whereabouts. China is a very large place, and my search could take months."

"And it could take half the time if I'm helping!"

"Ha! You tell him, boy," Dr. Mikolaitis put in.

"A possibility," said Mr. Scant. "But help me or hinder me, the point is moot. It is too far away, too uncertain, and too dangerous. My word is final."

I wanted to argue, but we were in danger of making a scene. "I'm going to look around."

"Don't go far," said Mr. Scant. "Stay where I can see you."

"I can look after myself. I don't need you watching over me. Isn't that what you wanted?"

"I already have two injured children making trouble for me. I don't need a third."

I walked away as Uncle Reggie sputtered his objection to being called a child. The ferry was big, with places to eat and relax and all manner of interesting rooms belowdecks, but despite what I had said, I decided not to stray too far from the others. Instead, I went to walk around the wide open deck.

The English Channel was a gray-blue tapestry laid out between us and the horizon, which itself may or may not have held a glimpse of white cliffs. Bright gems embroidered the water, glinting just for a moment as they caught the sun before vanishing again. The Channel looked bluer than it had on our way to France, when the lack of sunshine had made the tapestry look more like a lumpy gray bedsheet. On one side of the boat, a boy a little older than me was learning over the rail, presumably seasick, with his mother beside him, rubbing his back. I felt a pang of sympathy, but more than that, I wondered what he could see. I went over to the edge of the deck and, gripping the handrail tightly, looked over the edge.

The ferry carved its way through the water at a speed that was almost imperceptible when looking out toward Dover. Looking down, however, made for a bracing view, as the bulk of metal sliced its way through the salt water, cleaving it and tossing it carelessly behind. I could hear it too, the sound of the ferry forging its path, and felt I knew just for a moment why so many Englishmen found the call of life on the ocean wave irresistible.

I teetered as precariously as I dared over the rail, relishing the feeling of the salt air. When I leaned back and stretched my back in a satisfied way, I realized someone was beside me. I looked side to side and then down.

"Victor?" I said. The little boy grinned.

My shock quickly subsided. The determination on Victor's face back in Paris had made me almost expect something like this would happen. And now here he stood, in my clothes, sleeves and trouser legs still rolled up and pinned to look like they fit him better than they did. His brother's grubby shirt was half-hidden under my smallest waistcoat, topped with the large neckerchief Uncle Reggie had given him. He had managed to procure a white sailor's cap from somewhere or other, with *Marine Nationale* stitched into the front and a red pom-pom on the top. With his clean hair and my clothes, he couldn't have looked more different from when I had first seen him outside the Panthéon.

"What are you doing here?" I demanded.

"Ollie Olivier!" said a happy Victor.

I did the only thing I could think of, taking the boy by the wrist and marching him to Mr. Scant, who also didn't look particularly surprised but gave Victor a stern enough look that the boy began to explain. I couldn't follow what he was saying, but at one point Dr. Mikolaitis guffawed until the pain of his wound made him stop.

"What did he say?" I asked.

Mr. Scant rubbed his chin thoughtfully. "It seems that our cunning little gamin sat on the back of our carriage until we reached the docks, then simply said his mother and father were on board with his papers and ticket. Nobody thought to question such a well-dressed, polite little child. Of course a child that age had been accompanied by adults, they thought. Otherwise, how would he have gotten here?"

"So he stowed away?"

"It would appear so."

"What are we going to do? We have to take him back."

"You could ask the captain, but I'm not sure he'd be so keen to turn around," Uncle Reggie said with a grin.

"The boy wants to find his brother," said Dr. Mikolaitis. "He has nobody else in the world and thinks you're the only one who will help him. You've picked up a fine stray kitten, Master Oliver, and I think you'd better keep him safe."

"You're enjoying this, aren't you?" I said. "Both of you."

"It is a little funny," said Uncle Reggie, "but I do feel for the lad. He's completely alone. How would you feel in his situation?"

"Mr. Scant, what should we do?"

"What *can* we do, Master Oliver?"

I held my temples. "Isn't this illegal? Are we kid-napping him? No, I know, I know, there's nobody who's going to come looking for him. But surely we can't just take him away from his home?"

"He won't be missed," said Dr. Mikolaitis. "He only had his brother, and no home, no orphanage."

"But we can't take him home with *us*, can we?"

"Hmm," Uncle Reggie said, "all things consid-ered, that's probably a better choice than dumping him overboard. And he does seems very attached to you."

I looked back at Victor, who was holding onto the back of my jacket and peering around me at the unfamiliar men.

"Mr. Scant, I really don't know what to do," I said.

"Well, Master Oliver, you can take this as a lesson in not giving chocolate bonbons to waifs and strays, but beyond that, I would say it's now your responsi-bility to look after the lad. At least until we get home and can think of what best to do with him."

"Take him home?" I said. All of a sudden, the Diplexito residence in Tunbridge Wells seemed all

too real, no longer a vague idea at the end of an interesting trip but a looming and inevitable problem.
"But what's Mother going to say?"

Greatly to my surprise, what Mother said was, "Oh,
who is this darling little fellow? And Oliver, is that
your jacket from Wilton's he's wearing?"

"I . . . Yes, Mother."

"Doesn't he look a little angel in it? It was getting
too small for you, anyway. I'll get Penny to take it up
at the sleeves properly. Did you know she's good at
that sort of thing? Hello! Who are you?"

"Hello!" Victor said and struck his chest proudly
with his palm. "Victor!"

"Why, hello there, Victor! Don't you just look
like the sweetest duckling in your little sailor hat?"

"Ollie! *Maman!*" said Victor.

"He doesn't speak much English," I said.

"Oh, I see," Mother said before picking Victor up
and carrying him on her hip, saying hello again in
French, which she could speak well. I failed to follow
exactly the words she spoke next, but she turned to
her maid, Mrs. Winton, and said, "See if you can

find some of Oliver's old indoor shoes, won't you? There should be some in the storeroom." Then she looked back at Victor, and they laughed together. I felt a strange pang of old memories, while Victor beamed at Mother like he had been given a Christmas present. I wondered when he had last been held like that, if ever he had.

That was when Mother caught sight of Uncle Reggie and Dr. Mikolaitis being eased out of a large carriage, one we had hired because it was big enough that the two of them could stay supine in the wheeled beds we had rented in Dover. "What on Earth happened here?" she asked Mr. Scant. "Oliver, your tutor . . . And this is your brother, isn't it, Scant? We met at Christmas."

"Yes indeed. There was some unfortunate business in France, ma'am. These two were caught up in some sort of student demonstration. You know how violent the French can get. The police were involved."

"Sounds frightful," Mother said. She turned to Uncle Reggie and then Dr. Mikolaitis. "Please do take the time to recuperate here. I'll arrange for Dr. Webb to come and treat you."

"Much obliged, Mrs. Diplexito," said Uncle Reggie. "Please don't trouble yourself. My brother

Heck is all the nurse we need. He's a capable one, if not especially gentle."

"You weren't hurt at all, rabbit?"

"Please don't call me that," I said, squirming a little. "Nothing happened to me."

To my relief, that was all Mother asked. I felt a little guilty, but she was still in the dark about the incident with the Woodhouselee Society, Mr. Scant's history, his secret identity as the Ruminating Claw, and my own adventures. As far as she was aware, while in France, I had been on an educational trip.

"I hope you have time for nursing, Scant," Mother said. "It's been dreadful without you, but we muddled along. The girls try their best but can't get the hang of the Earl Grey. Do prepare us a proper afternoon tea, will you?"

"Of course, ma'am."

"And some Victoria sponge for the little one, I think." Mother grinned at Victor, who she was still carrying in her arms. "Children love a bit of sponge cake."

"Bitter spun cake!" Victor parroted.

I helped Mr. Scant wheel Uncle Reggie and Dr. Mikolaitis to the back of the house and through the French windows. We settled the two of them in the conservatory before going back to help with the luggage. Victor had distracted Meg and Penny; the maids cooed over him, playing with the pom-pom on the hat he still had on his head, even indoors. Even so, when they caught sight of me, they greeted me brightly. "You look taller," said Meg. "Or maybe I just didn't notice you growing until you went away."

In addition to all his other duties, Mr. Scant tended to act as our porter, and once he and the driver had brought in my trunks, Meg and Penny shooed me out, insisting they could sort my clothes better on their own. I went to find Mother, who was proudly showing off her piano-playing to a rapt Victor. I waited patiently for her to finish her Beethoven and gave her some polite applause, which Victor imitated.

"Well then," she said, modestly waving her hand to stop us clapping, "you've obviously had quite the adventure. Two men, black and blue, and one little French guest here who must miss his mother dearly."

"I don't think he has a mother," I said.

"Oh dear! Well, I'll hear the whole story, but wait until dinner so you don't have to repeat it for Father. You were safe, though, I trust?"

"I was with Mr. Scant," I said, which was answer enough.

For his part, Mr. Scant seemed to be avoiding me. He busied himself first with unpacking and then, in Father's study, going through his paperwork and appointments, making notes and rearranging things. When I tried to ask him what was going to happen next, he simply said, "I have my valet's duties, Master Oliver, and you ought to look over your schoolwork before your next lesson."

"I finished my schoolwork. You made me finish it before we went to France!"

"Then may I suggest checking and double-checking it?"

By that time, Victor had fallen asleep in the guest room that Mother and old Mrs. Winton had arranged for him. His sailor hat was hanging from one corner of the headboard, while a pair of my old indoor shoes were waiting at the foot of the bed.

"He misses his brother very much," Mother said. "He says bad men took the poor chap off to China, but I'm not sure I understood all of it. Kept talking about men with a big gun. I think he has quite the imagination, and of course the poor little sweetling was falling asleep as he talked. He speaks very highly of you, though!"

"Says you were like an angel," said Mrs. Winton.

"Course, he hasn't seen the things we have."

Mother laughed, then sat on the bed and beckoned me over. Victor grumbled in his sleep and turned over as I sat down, but he didn't wake.

"He looks a little like you did when you were that age," Mother observed. "Only you were more of a rabbit, and he's more of a mouse. We'll look after him for as long as we need to, though of course he must get back to his brother as soon as possible. I asked Mrs. George if she could make French food, but she says she only knows about snails and frogs. I hope the boy isn't too picky."

"I think he's learned to just eat whatever he's given."

"Ah, a well-mannered boy."

"I suppose so."

"Have you seen Mrs. George?" Mother asked. "She was very much looking forward to your return."

"No, I should go and say hello. When's Father home?"

"For dinner, if not before. What time is it now?"

Mrs. Winton consulted a pocket watch. "A quarter to four."

"Another hour or two," Mother said. "He's looking forward to seeing you too."

"Honestly?" I asked.

"Honestly."

As promised, I went to visit Mrs. George in her kitchens. She shrieked like a banshee at the sight of me and took me in a suffocating hug that would have gotten her dismissed from a stricter household. "The girls tell me that Mr. Gaunt decided to shoot the Russian fella but only got a good walloping for his trouble, and then you kidnapped a French baby."

"I . . . what? That's not right," I said with a laugh, unsure if the twins had been confused or if Mrs. George had misunderstood. "Uncle Reggie was beaten up by some hired hands, and someone from the Society shot Dr. Mikolaitis in the leg. But they're alright. Well, not alright exactly, but they'll get better."

Mrs. George nodded thoughtfully. Unlike Mother, Mrs. George had been along for the ride when we battled the Woodhouselee Society, so I had no secrets from her. "I'll whip them up some chicken soup," she said. "That always helps."

"I'm not sure it helps gunshot wounds."

"It helps *everything*," Mrs. George said sagely.

"If you say so. As for Victor, he's not a baby—he's

nine or ten. And we didn't kidnap him. He followed us. He stowed away on the ferry!"

"Sounds like a piece of work. And now he wants a sponge cake, I hear."

"Well, I think that was Mother's idea."

"Not to worry," Mrs. George said, "I was making one anyway, for you. With custard. I know how you love it."

I smiled. "Can't say no to a bit of custard."

Mrs. George laced her fingers together and pushed out her wrists so that her knuckles cracked. "I'm making such a dinner as you'll never forget. Just waiting for a few more things to be delivered. But first, let's go and see everyone. I can't go gallivanting around the house on my own, but if you ask me to come with you, dear, dear Master Oliver, it won't be a problem."

"I don't see why not."

So I took Mrs. George to see our guests. Dr. Mikolaitis kissed her hand while looking exaggeratedly doleful. She laughed and promised him some vodka after dinner. Uncle Reggie greeted her like an old friend and told her all about how he had heroically fought off ten men before a "scoundrel crept up and coshed me from behind." Mrs. George nodded sympathetically.

"So if he gets vodka, do I get a nice single malt?" Uncle Reggie asked.

"You'll get a fresh lump on your head if you carry on like that," said Mrs. George. "But I'll see what I can scrounge up. Now, where's this little one? I want to see him."

"Victor's upstairs," I said. "I'll take you to see him."

But before I could lead her to the staircase, we heard voices in the hallway. Deep and resonant, the kind of voices that came from thick barrel chests by way of very bushy beards.

"Father's home!" I said, and ran out to meet him, with Mrs. George following behind, trying to tidy herself up.

In the hallway, Mr. Scant was helping Father out of his coat, another coat already draped over his arm. "Father!" I called, and then noticed the owner of the other coat. "And Mr. Beards!"

"There he is!" Father said, chuckling as I hurried over to embrace him. It was strange to remember how only a year ago, Father would barely acknowledge my presence, let alone greet me so happily. But things had changed since we foiled Mr. Binns's plans.

"I'm so happy to be back," I said. "Hello, Mr. Beards."

"A very good day to you, Master Diplexito," Mr. Beards said, with a twitch of his whiskers. He was an old-fashioned sort, and I knew he had been having a difficult time since the business he ran with Mr. Binns collapsed. But he had started an airship business with most of his former employees just two months later and was now partnered with Father. Father had confided that the old man was effectively an employee—Diplexito Engineering, Tunbridge Wells, had put up all the money for the new business—but that he and Mr. Beards had been partners for such a long time it wouldn't do to change the relationship.

"I have such a lot to tell you," I said, before noticing Mrs. George standing by the wall in a very respectful posture. "Ah," I continued, "I invited Mrs. George up with me to see the guests. There's a lot to explain."

"Plenty of time for that, my lad," Father said. "And this is convenient. Mrs. George, Beards will be staying for dinner, so one more, please."

"Yes sir," said Mrs. George, with an awkward little curtsy.

At that moment, Mother came down the main staircase, with Mrs. Winton behind her. "Darling, you're home! Welcome back. And Mr. Beards, a pleasure as always. I do hope you're stopping for dinner. How is Deidre?"

Mr. Beards kissed Mother's hand as she arrived. "You look charming as always, Edwina. It will be my pleasure to stay for the evening. And Deidre sends her love. She's been down with a bad throat the last few days, but it will pass soon, Dr. Bordon says. Gerty fancies herself a nurse these days and has been taking care of her."

Mother nodded. "I do hope she recovers quickly. We missed her on crochet night."

"Now," Father said to Mr. Scant, some steps away from Mother, "Let's have all the news from France in the study. Don't hold anything back because Beards is here. He knows all the ins and outs, don't you worry."

Mr. Scant bowed his head a little and made for the study, but before he reached the door, he was stopped by a piercing scream.

"What the devil was that?" asked Father.

"Victor," I said, and after meeting Mr. Scant's eye for a moment, we went running in the direction of the boy's voice.

VI

Blood and Custard

We found Victor in the downstairs corridor, curled up in fear. He was on the floor in my old bedclothes, trying to squeeze himself through the skirting board in his attempt to get away from the fearsome sight before him.

Desperately trying to calm the boy by waving her huge hands at him—an assortment of animal parts poking gruesomely out of the small bag she carried on her shoulder—was the Valkyrie. I had never seen her look as troubled as she did in her efforts to shush the boy.

"Ah, it's you," Mr. Scant said, narrowing his eyes at the former agent of the Woodhouselee Society, now peacefully employed in her father's butcher shop.

When Victor saw us, he scrambled up and came running to me, beginning to blub again. Father appeared with the others, demanding to know what was happening, and Victor hopped from foot to foot as he tried to decide whom to hide from. Looking back at the Valkyrie, who tried to raise a smile for him, he decided she was definitely the most fearsome of all.

"I didn't mean to make a scene," the Valkyrie said, looking at us like an overgrown child caught doing something mischievous. "I think I must have surprised the little one."

"Matilda Troughton!" Mrs. George barked. "Just what do you think you're doing?" She turned to Father and bobbed a little curtsy. "Begging your pardon, sir, if I may have a word with her?" When Father nodded, Mrs. George gave a quick jab of her thumb toward the door the Valkyrie must have come through and then led the other woman to the kitchen stairs.

"Shh, you're alright," I said to Victor. He had buried his face in my side, which would have seemed sweeter had so many parts of that face not been leaking various fluids.

"So this is—" Father began, but he was interrupted by Mrs. George's voice, which a closed door did little to muffle.

"I know I wasn't in the kitchen, Matilda!" she was yelling. "You could have waited for me there instead of stomping about, putting the fear of God into our little guest!"

Father cleared his throat and, more loudly, went on. "So this is the little French lad, eh? Come on, little fellow, you see one big girl and you start blubbing? Show a bit of pluck!"

I looked back at him in irritation. "Victor doesn't speak English. And he just got a bit startled. The Val—er, I mean, Miss Troughton is about four times his size."

Father looked back to Victor, who had sidled back around me, and spoke in a slow, clear voice—as though that would make him completely comprehensible to a little boy who knew only French. "If you think she's scary now, you should have seen her when she was trying to rip people's arms off. Rip!"

He mimed a rather alarming gesture and pointed to the door, but that only had the effect of making Victor begin to whine. Mother swept forward.

"Why don't we try being delicate?" she said. She seemed a little puzzled too, presumably because she had never known the Valkyrie as we had, so Father's words meant nothing to her. She knelt in front of

Victor, speaking to him softly in French. He nodded but didn't let go of me.

"Delicate?" said Father. "Well, worth a try, perhaps. But boys need to be tough, eh, Oliver?"

"I suppose so, Father," I said. "But I think it's probably fine to be frightened of the Valkyrie when you're little."

"Well, he's calming down now, at least."

"I told him Miss Troughton is nothing to be afraid of," said Mother. "You shouldn't give her beastly nicknames, you hear me, Oliver? Her name is Miss Troughton, not 'the Valkyrie.' In fact, I think it would be good to invite Miss Troughton to share our dinner tonight."

"That colossus, at my dinner table?" Father caught Mother's eye, and his expression suddenly changed. "Oh. Ah. Capital idea. Right. Scant! I'll leave the arrangements to you."

⚜

Dinner was a polite affair. Around the table sat Father and Mother, Mr. Beards, and myself, with Victor by my side and, opposite him, a fidgeting Valkyrie. She towered over the rest of us seated for the meal, and over some of the staff standing up too. Four of the dining chairs had been moved aside to allow Dr. Mikolaitis and Uncle Reggie to join us on their wheeled beds, which could be adjusted to place the men upright. The twins served the lamb that the Valkyrie had brought with her, which Mrs. George had prepared with remarkable speed, and though Victor sniffed it suspiciously before trying it, he found it most agreeable.

We talked about the trip to France, but as Mother was there, kept it mainly to the educational blessings of a day at the Louvre. Uncle Reggie had enormous fun making up a tall tale to explain his injuries, revolving around his interrupting a robbery at a jewelry store. His story took us up until dessert, which turned out to be apple and pear crumble with custard. Victor ate his with gleaming eyes, and when he began to use his finger to wipe up every last trace of custard, I pushed my bowl sideways so he could finish mine as well. The boy let out a little whine of joy and whispered in his best attempt at English, "Thank you!"

After the meal, when Mother had retired, Father had another word with Mr. Scant, who had begun to wheel his brother toward Father's study. Mr. Scant met the Valkyrie's eye, and she seemed to realize he wanted something from her, so she offered to help with Dr. Mikolaitis's chair.

"Right then," Father said. "Miss Troughton, please do stay. We may need your opinion on a thing or two. Gentlemen, please rest assured you can speak freely in front of Beards. Now, let's sort this thing out. Scant, what happened in France?"

As Mr. Scant told the full story, I looked around the strange group assembled in Father's study. There was Uncle Reggie and Dr. Mikolaitis, invalided in their reclining chairs. Mr. Beards listened with his eyes closed, one hand stroking the white beard that so neatly matched his name, perhaps to show he was awake. Victor remained at my side, occasionally rubbing his belly in satisfaction. And the Valkyrie loomed above us all uncomfortably, clearly unsure what she was meant to do.

After Mr. Scant finished, Father nodded as though processing the new information. "So, to summarize," he said, "even with Binns locked up, the Society isn't done with. Beards, do you remember this Binns boy?"

"Oh yes, I remember him, but back when he was a slip of a lad," said Mr. Beards. "They packed him off to boarding school very young. 'Aurelian'—odd name. Thomasina's choice. Funny story about that, once I—"

"No time for funny stories now, Beards," Father said. "Miss Troughton, wasn't it?"

The Valkyrie responded as if in a schoolhouse. "Yes, sir?"

"You were an important member of the Wood-houselee Society. Have they contacted you?"

"I was only there for the fighting, sir."

"Hmm," said Father.

"If I may," said Dr. Mikolaitis, his voice strong despite his injury, "you didn't answer the question."

"Doesn't make it any less true," Miss Troughton said, giving him a sharp look, and just for a moment the old Valkyrie was there again, ready to fight. "They'd never tell me more about a plan than I needed to know. But yes. Yes, since the big scrap and Mr. Binns getting locked up, I've been asked to fight some more. I said no."

"Asked by whom?" said Mr. Scant.

"It wasn't just by one person. But I told them all no."

"Was one of them Mr. Binns' son?" I asked. "Um, Aurelian?"

"He came, yes," the Valkyrie said, with a solemn nod and a nervous look at Mr. Beards. "Not many of them frightened me, but he did. He didn't want me for more fighting. He said I was a failure, too weak to help. He just came to threaten me, said I'd better not talk to Scotland Yard and make things any worse for his family than they already are, or something might happen to Mum and Dad."

"Dr. Mikolaitis, do you know anything about this boy?" said Father.

"Not at all. That is, I knew he existed—but for all I knew, he was a simple schoolboy. Nobody ever mentioned him in my time with the Society."

"Miss Troughton, I want to hear about the other times you were approached by members of the Society," said Father. "Can you tell us about the others?"

"Yes," the Valkyrie said and then took her glass of water from Mr. Scant. "Thank you. There were four times in total, including the boy's visit. The other men were scared and desperate. They threatened, pleaded, tried to make a bargain, but none of them had a real plan other than try to pretend things were the way they used to be. All of them brought big men with them. But the Binns boy, he came alone, and he wasn't scared. I don't think he was a fighter. He just didn't seem to care about getting hurt or being apprehended and arrested. Nothing. He was cold. He made me feel like he had come to completely under-stand the world and decided it was a rotten place. It's hard to explain."

"I think the real question we need answered is what he has planned," said Uncle Reggie. "Any ideas?"

"He didn't tell me," said the Valkyrie. "He just told me there would be a new Society and I was not welcome. I think he said it would be a force to be reckoned with, not just a make-believe club. That I should never forget I betrayed his mother and father."

"In other words, watch your back," said Dr. Miko-laitis. "But as of now, it's all talk. Just words. No?"

"Hrmm," said Father, nodding. "What do you think, Scant?"

Mr. Scant nodded his head courteously at being acknowledged. "Well, sir, from what Monsieur Ber-nard and Miss Troughton have said, we can deduce that while the Woodhouselee Society has been fractured, certain factions are still hoping to use the contacts made by your erstwhile business partner to further their own goals. And most prominent of these would appear to be Mr. Binns the Younger, who I strongly suspect was also behind the assault on my brother."

Mr. Scant gave a sideways look to Uncle Reggie. "Now, unfortunately, the destination on the crate and the individuals we met during the incident in Gravesend with the land ironclad suggest to me that strong links have been made between the revived Society and a certain criminal organization in China. Moreover, Reginald's daughter, Miss Elspeth Gaunt, may have been in some way recruited by an organization working to thwart the criminals—possibly from within. And we also must consider the possibility that she is in fact part of the Tri-Loom now."

At this, Uncle Reggie frowned but did not interrupt.

"We have no decisive evidence that Elspeth has found her way overseas," Mr. Scant continued, "but Madame Curie informed us that Elspeth had not been finishing her studies at Sèvres, as we'd once believed. And the Binns boy told Reggie she'd be in China before trying to send him there too. Now, it's entirely possible this was a lie to mislead us, and Elspeth is instead working secretly somewhere in Europe.

"Crucial, in all of this: the last time we saw Elspeth, she partnered with one Miss Cai Zhao-Ji, as agents of an organization we know even less about than we do the Society. So we must ask ourselves: could Miss Cai Zhao-Ji's commanding officers have summoned her back to her homeland? Was dismantling the Society her only goal here in England? And if she has gone back to China, might Elspeth have joined her?"

"I didn't want any of this to happen," Uncle Reggie said dolefully. "And I don't know why they wanted to ship me off to China, either."

"Another mystery," said Mr. Scant. "Of course, you were not going as a free man, and there was probably a very specific fate waiting for you, but why go to such lengths? It's possible that everything was an elaborate ruse, set up with the intention of us finding and freeing Reginald, with the mention of China a careful misdirection. But it seems to me the probability of our failing was too high for that to be the case."

"Even if we're being manipulated," Uncle Reggie began, "what choice do I have? They say that Ellie is in China, so I need to go and fetch her."

"You're in no state to go anywhere," said Father.

Dr. Mikolaitis laughed and added, "Going to limp all the way there and hit the Tri-Loom with your crutches?"

"Don't underestimate a father's love," said Uncle Reggie. "What's an ocean or two to a father whose daughter is in danger? Ellie is only sixteen! Sixteen years old, halfway across the world, and mixed up with all this secret society business." He looked askance at the doctor. "I know what you're thinking, don't think I can't tell. 'He lets the Society take his daughter away for ten years or more and he now wants to call himself a father.' Well, I know it better than anyone. I do! And I'm going to fight twice as hard because of my past mistakes."

"Nobody is doubting your resolve, Gaunt," Father said, with a hint of irritation. "But you're in a bad state, and you'll be worse off if you go gallivanting off around the world. What do you suppose you can do to help this girl of yours while you're dead on your feet?"

Uncle Reggie said nothing, but it was clear from the look in his eyes his mind was made up.

"We also need to decide what to do about Victor," I said. "He's very worried about his older brother, Julien."

At the mention of Julien's name, Victor stopped playing with the fabric of Father's study chair and let loose a rapid stream of French. Rather than answering him, Father looked to Mr. Scant.

"What do you suppose has happened to his brother?"

"We can only guess, Sir," said Mr. Scant. "But if Julien vanished in the same place as we found Reginald, well, there were a lot of other crates there marked *SHANGHAI* . . ."

Victor hit his little hands on Father's desk and spoke again, directing most of his speech to Mr. Scant—he'd quickly figured out who among us could understand him and who would only give him blank stares. Mr. Scant translated. "He says he's sure his brother is in Shanghai; he heard the men talking about it. I'm not clear on which men these may be. He says he's going to find his brother. No matter what."

"All signs point to Shanghai," said Father. "But it's not a quick ferry ride across the Channel." He let out a deep breath. "Let's lay it all out. Gaunt here is determined to go and find his daughter, who may or may not be in China, as the Binns boy intimated. But he's on death's door. The child here heard his brother is in China too, from persons unknown, speaking French—which in my book is reason enough to doubt everything they say, but that's by the by. Well, it seems to me *someone* has to make the trip, no?" He stroked his beard and then shrugged. "I did without a valet during your excursion to France, Scant. I suppose it will have to be you."

"I don't know how long it would take me, Sir."

"I know, I know. I'll have to get by. Can you entrust this to your brother, Gaunt?"

"Hmmph. Grudgingly," Uncle Reggie said.

Once Mr. Scant had translated this development for Victor, Victor created a commotion in response, yelling, "*Non, non, non!*" He rushed over to me and grabbed my sleeve.

"Victor assumes he's going to China," Mr. Scant explained. "But he won't go without Master Oliver."

Victor looked at me with eyes big as saucers—just-washed saucers at that, because they glistened as the tears formed. He said something in a very high, tight voice.

"He says he wants you to help him," said Mr. Scant.

"I want to," I said. "I want to go! But . . . what about school?"

"As your tutor, I could prepare lessons and give them to dear Mr. Scant," said Dr. Mikolaitis, with a smirk. "I'm sure he'd make a very strict teacher. Besides, you'll learn more traveling the world than you will in a few weeks at school."

"I . . . did learn a lot in France," I said.

"You also saw a fellow get shot," said Father. "It doesn't sound like fun and games."

"As long as Mr. Scant's with me, I'm not afraid," I said.

"I think I can make arrangements with the school," said Father. "It's not so uncommon for children to have to travel for a time."

"Perhaps the Valkyrie herself could join you?" said Dr. Mikolaitis.

"Me?" said Miss Troughton. "Oh, no, no, I couldn't. If you need me here, I'll come at a snap of the fingers. I'm in your debt for not turning me in to the Yard. But I can't just leave the shop and go to China."

"You have your duties, and we won't keep you from them," said Father. "I suppose, then, I'm sending my only son off to the other side of the world. Scant, you'd best keep him safe."

"I swear it on my life, Sir."

"That's what I like to hear. Now how will we get you there?"

"Ah!"

We all turned to Mr. Beards, who I had all but forgotten was there.

"This is where I can help," he said triumphantly. "If it's a long journey you're wanting, there's only one thing for it. An airship!"

VII

To Shanghai

Beards's eyes were brighter than sapphires as he spoke about the future of dirigibles, of how the skies would soon be crowded with them bumping and buffeting against one another, and how the Royal Navy was building airships that would put the Germans to shame even as we spoke. Even so, we soon learned flying all the way to China in one go was impossible—the most ambitious aeronauts had travelled only about half that distance.

Nonetheless, Mr. Scant, Victor, and I boarded Mr. Beards's airship, *Oberon*, along with Beards himself. The ship was emblazoned with *Beards and Binns Dirigibles*, but with *and Binns* hastily and inadequately painted over. Other than this blemish, the ship was a fine sight to behold. However, actually stepping aboard the thing filled me with a sense of foreboding.

It was not so much that we were leaving behind England and friends and loved ones and schoolwork and readily available tea, but the fact that I had not the faintest inkling what awaited us at our destination. China was on the other side of the world, and to me, a place of fairy tales. Mr. Scant archly told me that the China I had read about in the story of Aladdin was nothing like what we would see in Shanghai.

Riding in the airship was an odd experience, much like being at sea, though when the wind blew hard, it was even more terrifying than a great wave catching a ferry. We cleaved a path through the clouds, up above the grayness, which, once underneath us, looked solid enough to stand upon. The capacious *Oberon* was far more comfortable than the hot-air balloon in which I'd ridden some months back, but of course we would be stuck inside the airship for far longer. Victor had apparently been unprepared for the length of the journey, but we had brought many English picture books and board games with which he could pass the time.

We travelled for six days in this manner, stopping several times to gather supplies and so our pilot, Mr. Beards, could sleep. I developed a habit of sleeping while we were in the air, as Mr. Beards was prone to loud snores. Our sense of the time of day gradually left us as we crossed the globe. I developed a habit of sitting by the iron door, where I fancied there was a very slight breeze, though Mr. Beards told me it was from the sophisticated air-circulation system and not from outside. Meanwhile, Mr. Scant had grown serious about his new role as an educator, and I spent much of the trip reading *The Pilgrim's Progress*, memorizing declensions, and perusing a history of China, found on short notice, that ended in 1644.

Mr. Beards flew us to Egypt, making a point of flying low over the ancient pyramids before we landed at the Suez Canal. He also shared stories of having lived in Africa for a time when he was a young man. I had difficulty imagining Mr. Beards as a young man, and even when I imagined him as a child, he always had that same puffy white beard. From that point onward, the airship was packed onto a steamer, which took us on to Bombay. Our route, I noted, was very similar to that taken by Mr. Fogg in *Around the World in Eighty Days*, only with an airship. Things had progressed since Mr. Verne had written that book, so our progress was swifter—it took us only nine days in total to reach India, with plenty of stops for provisions and bathing.

There, we were met by a contact of Father's named Mr. Siddiqui, who was very accommodating and gave us delicious sweet tea and even had some custard for Victor. He had the equipment to re-inflate *Oberon* and graciously restocked our provisions. He even gave Victor a small square hat decorated in jewels Mr. Siddiqui had worn for a durbar—which I gathered was some sort of important event for the old king—which Victor happily exchanged for his French sailor's cap. Our host also asked after Mother, and it pained me slightly to remember how bewildered she had been that Father had insisted I begin an educational venture in China so soon after my trip to France.

As he had intended from the outset, Mr. Beards stayed with Mr. Siddiqui and his acquaintances to discuss new business deals. This meant Mr. Scant was entrusted with the dirigible's controls. Of course, Mr. Scant showed no sign of apprehension, but the journey was noticeably bumpier than before.

"Can't you keep things steady?" I asked Mr. Scant after a particularly large lurch sent Victor and me tumbling against the table where Mr. Scant had laid out a map.

"I'm doing my best, Master Oliver. This isn't as simple as it may seem."

The journey to Shanghai took several more days, and the next time we stopped to make camp, we barely saw a soul. Those who came to take curious looks at the airship quickly rushed away if they saw us, which was a shame because they looked like they would be interesting people with stories to tell, though likely not in English. During the trip's last leg, I struggled to discern when India became China, so it almost took me by surprise when we reached Shanghai.

Unlike our stop in India, there was nobody to meet us when we reached Shanghai. Mr. Scant left the airship in a dockyard, locked the gondola door, and simply walked away from the vehicle. "Should we not deflate it?" I asked.

"We don't know how long we will be here, whether the balloon will be stolen the moment it can be hauled away, or whether the locals will be honor-bound to leave it untouched. We may even need to make a hasty escape. If the authorities question us, would we be able to explain our situation? For my part, I know not one single word of Chinese, be it Cantonese or Shanghainese. I have been studying the writing, but with no one to tell me the sounds, I was unable to learn the spoken language. I do apologize for this lack of foresight."

"So we're just going to leave the airship there and hope for the best?"

"Yes, Master Oliver. Though from what I read on the way here, people may not be so happy to see the foreign dirigible. Or, indeed, the foreigners from inside it."

It didn't take long to understand what Mr. Scant had meant by this. As we walked from the river into the city proper, I began to appreciate we were in a place far more unfamiliar and bewildering than the streets of Paris. My French may have been limited, but at least I could read the signs around me and have a good stab at pronouncing the words. Here, there was plentiful lettering on the flags and shop signs, but I couldn't read a single character.

The locals all stared at as we passed, especially at Victor, with his long, unruly hair spilling out from under the little square hat Mr. Siddiqui had given him. Some of the people watching us seemed curious and nodded in greeting, but most frowned or looked away as though they had seen something distasteful. People dressed differently and moved differently here, and I realized I had—perhaps stupidly—expected everybody to be the same age. I anticipated a country full of men of about thirty-five years old, dressed in silk Chinese jackets with their hair in a braid called a *queue*. But there was the same variety in Shanghai as anywhere else in the world—men and women, young and old, slender and portly, well-groomed and unkempt. Children came running to look at us, and the elderly with bent backs glanced up at us as they shuffled past. Some men wore Chinese-style shirts with the knots instead of buttons, but others were clothed in Western-style jackets or suits. Many of them did wear their hair in queues, but others had their hair cut short, and those locals seemed to be the ones who scrutinized us most closely.

"Why are they so suspicious of us?" I asked, as a rickshaw clattered past.

"That's rather a long story, Master Oliver," said Mr. Scant. "Are you not too hot in your jacket?"

"It's a little warm, but I'm fine."

"If you remove your jacket, young Master Victor will do the same, and I think he will be more comfortable."

Amused that Mr. Scant had called him "Master Victor" instead of "the boy" or "the urchin," I looked down at Victor, who, as though on cue, squirmed uncomfortably in his jacket and tugged at his collar. I helped him out of his jacket, handing it to Mr. Scant, but for my part, I kept my jacket on. I wanted to make a good impression.

"Now, Mr. Scant," I said, turning the conversation back to the suspicion that seemed to encircle us, "we have time for a long story, don't we?"

"I'm not sure, Master Oliver," said Mr. Scant. "I'm rather hoping that if we walk around conspicuously, at some point we will be accosted by somebody who speaks English and wants to know our business. Though, short of that, our first port of call ought to be the embassy."

"I don't have the sense they're staring just because they haven't seen foreigners before."

"Indeed not," said Mr. Scant. "Shanghai is an important port city. A considerable amount of trade takes place here. I'm sure these citizens have seen visitors from more countries than the people of Tunbridge Wells. French, German, Italian, Japanese, American."

"Americans?" I said. "Do you think we'll see cowboys?"

"I . . . can't rule it out," said Mr. Scant.

"Goodness," I said. As we reached the thick of the city, fragrant smoke billowed out of vents above dark windows like mists from the North York Moors, and stall owners called out to passersby in loud voices like the vendors in Borough Market. Still, there was no mistaking Shanghai for England. Horse-drawn carriages clattered past, but most people seemed to career by us either in rickshaws or on small platforms around the front wheel of some sort of adapted wheelbarrows.

"If foreigners are so common, why are they staring at us?" I asked.

"From what I read in preparation for the journey, this is a tense time. The country is on the brink of revolution."

"Revolution?" I asked. "Like in France? That would be terrible. A lot of people died."

"Well, those who want revolution might tell you things are terrible now."

"They don't look so terrible."

"I don't suppose every street in Paris looked terrible before the fighting, either."

"You're scaring me a little," I said. When Mr. Scant made no reply, I added, "I still don't see what this has to do with the way they're looking at us."

"Unlike other great revolutions, the one on the horizon in China looks to be brought about by the presence of foreigners. And its wrath may reach foreigners as well." We rounded a corner onto a busier road, and a Westerner passed us, doffing his hat. Mr. Scant made a small bow, but the man hurried on without a word. With a disappointed sigh, Mr. Scant went on. "By the looks of things, we do have time for the longer version. You are probably aware of the so-called Opium Wars."

"I've heard of them."

"Not a pleasant business," Mr. Scant said. "I am no history teacher, but as the onus is upon me to act as a tutor, I will explain to the best of my ability. The Opium Wars were, in essence, a strategy to force trade on a nation that had never needed it. China is a large country that was quite able to feed its people, craft its own beautiful arts, and mine precious metals and jewels for the wealthy. Other countries coveted the materials created here, but what to trade to a country that needed nothing? And so these countries created a market—a market for opium. Weak-willed people put it in their pipes to forget the pain of their lives, but they're left with a still greater pain, and they need more and more."

"I've heard about addiction," I said. "And I'm not just talking about Victor and custard."

"Custard?" said Victor, looking around in excitement before I shook my head.

"The Chinese made opium illegal," Mr. Scant continued, "and refused to change this position even as its use became widespread. The people wanted opium, and they went to the British and Americans for it, even if selling it within their home country was punishable by death."

"It seems very wicked to use something like that just to have something to trade."

"Wicked, yes," said Mr. Scant, "but money is tempting, and after all, there were eager buyers. Very eager. The emperor himself took notice and sent an official to deal with the problem. The official decided to confiscate all the opium he could find from British merchants—more than a thousand tons. He had five hundred men work for more than three weeks to destroy it all and throw it into the sea. This did not sit well with the British merchants. Considering it theft, they brought in gunboats. The Chinese had great riches but next to no way to resist British naval power."

"Britannia rules the waves," I said. The words sounded bitter all of a sudden.

"Just so, Master Oliver. Then as now. And when the wars were over, the British could make whatever demands we wished. Millions upon millions of trade dollars were asked of the Chinese, to pay for the opium that was destroyed as well as for lost trade and the cost of the war. And then, on top of that, for favorable trading terms, including a huge port the British could control."

"Shanghai?"

"Ah, no. It's certainly open to foreigners today, but it's not a British colony. I speak of Hong Kong. And soon after came the inevitable legalization of the opium trade."

"I think I see why people might be suspicious of visitors," I said.

"Oh, but this is not the end of the story," Mr. Scant continued. "These wars took place a long time ago, and friendly trade has since flourished. Foreigners are not an uncommon sight in many cities like this one, and there is demand now for a wide variety of goods. But roughly ten years ago, a new conflict erupted. With trade opened, other Western countries came to China, seeking influence in this rich and important country. And with them came priests, spreading the word of Our Lord in a foreign land. After this, and plague, and droughts, the people of China grew angry. A kind of army was formed, called the Boxers."

"I've heard of them," I said. "The Boxer Rebellion?"

"Quite so. At first, the Boxers were rebels. But by 1900, when they gathered in Peking in great numbers and chased the eight or nine hundred foreigners here to one small district, the Empress Dowager Cixi— I'm afraid I am not certain if I am pronouncing that correctly—decided to declare war on all the foreign powers. At the time, I'm told she was more powerful than the emperor himself. But this time, the Chinese had forces beyond the British to contend with. There were Germans, Russians, even Japanese, all trapped in Peking and held as hostages."

"So what happened?"

"The hostages were rescued, at a great cost to their captors. Eight countries united against China. Many died. Peking was torn to pieces; every treasure that could be carried away was stolen. And again, China found itself in a position with no power to negotiate. The Eight-Nation Alliance demanded reparations once more. Which brings us to today, where we find China no longer the country of untold riches it once was. For ten years, China has been paying the foreign nations for the mistake of rising up against them. In some ways, China belongs to foreign powers. Empress Dowager Cixi passed away three years ago, in the autumn of 1908. But on her deathbed, she chose Emperor Xuantong, as I think it is said. The current emperor."

"Is he the little boy?"

"Indeed. Much younger than you or even the young French master. I believe the emperor is five or six years old—the Chinese consider you a year old at birth, counting the time in your mother's belly. The boy is not a leader and has no power to negotiate the debts of his country. That is why there is talk of revolution. Not because the boy is hated or cruel, but because of debt. Debts to foreign powers that derive from attempts to fight foreign powers."

"Poor boy."

"The emperor?"

"Yes," I said. "How can a little boy deal with problems like that? If he was born before all this, he would have had such a good life. Might have become a great leader. But now everything's such a mess. And it's not his fault."

"A sad situation," Mr. Scant said, "but one many kings and emperors must face."

I nodded. "So what about us? How do we find Elspeth or Julien?"

"I rather hoped we would have found someone to talk to by now."

"Oh, but you have," came a voice from behind us. Mr. Scant spun around, his hand going to his hip, prepared to reach for the claw. Someone creeping up on Mr. Scant was no common occurrence, but as I looked around, I saw how it had happened. Instead of walking behind us, he had ridden slowly on his bicycle, making next to no sound at all. The man from Notre Dame, the contact from Scotland Yard who had told us to call him Jackdaw.

"I do beg your pardon for not speaking up sooner," said Mr. Jackdaw. "I was rather enjoying your insight into the hairy mess we have now."

"We saw you in France," I said. "How did you get here?"

Mr. Jackdaw produced two bags of chocolate eggs, one for me and one for Victor, who opened his at once and started to feast. "We have our ways, don't you know? You certainly didn't choose the quickest method to get here, though I'm sure it was more comfortable than mine. Or perhaps I'm just an identical brother of the Jackdaw you met in France. But you must call me Jackdaw too."

"And I suppose we'll be going with you now."

"Oh yes." Mr. Jackdaw lifted his fingers in a kind of beckoning signal, in response to which four more men rode up behind him. Their own bicycles seemed almost absurdly small, because the men were so muscular. Though they were all Chinese, they wore Western-style shirts, the sleeves rolled up to reveal large, veiny forearms. "These are my friends, who will escort us to a nearby restaurant. Let's go and have some *xiao long bao.*"

VIII

Under the Bridge and Over

Mr. Jackdaw took us to a richly decorated restaurant in the basement of a large building in a Western style, designed as if a European town hall had been scooped up by some great cosmic hand and placed down here amidst the elegant pagodas and gilded temples. I felt a strange sense of kinship with that building, as if I had been placed here by that same hand.

Though there were no windows in the restaurant, the place was bright with electric lights, a feast for the eyes. Large wooden screens divided huge tables from one another, and large works of art decorated every wall. Most were wooden carvings of village scenes and mountains, but no more than four or five inches thick, so the pieces had the qualities of both sculpture and painting. A huge, golden

Chinese character hung behind the largest table, encircled by carved dragons with half-lizard, half-lion faces. This was the table Mr. Jackdaw led us to, as the owners of the restaurant greeted him like an old friend. He took his place under the Chinese character and then smiled at us warmly, showing us a strange set of teeth, white and straight but with tiny gaps between all of them.

"Have you ever tried a *xiao long bao*?" he began. "I prefer the *char siu bao* in Hong Kong, but these are the local specialty and really very good. I hope you're more open-minded than my colleagues. If I hear 'foreign muck' one more time, it will lead to fisticuffs."

He regarded Mr. Scant first, and then me.

"I've never tried one," I said.

"You're in for a treat." He turned Victor and repeated the question in French.

Victor pursed his lips and said, "*Mais Julien, où est-il?*"

Mr. Jackdaw said that he was very sorry but he didn't know where Julien could be found, or something along those lines. Then he looked back to me and Mr. Scant. "I'm sure you were surprised to see me. Putting aside that twin nonsense, you're wondering why I would have been sent to the other side of the world. Just to show you a friendly face? To give the impression the Yard is much more capable than you thought? Because it's amusing to watch you try to guess the motivation? Isn't it maddening?"

"Not really," said Mr. Scant. "It's obvious you're not going to give us an answer, and if you did, we would have no reason to believe it."

Mr. Jackdaw laughed. "Maybe you're right, and maybe you're wrong. How will you know if you don't ask? Ah, here come the *bao*. The service is so fast here."

The staff brought over several large round baskets made of some kind of wood, with lids that made them look like cooking pots. An inviting steam and still more inviting smell drifted out of the baskets as they were placed in the center of the table. Then the lids were removed, revealing a number of small dumplings with the look of sugar icing to them, closed at the top with a little swirl. A pretty girl in a shimmering dress distributed bowls, chopsticks, and large white spoons to each of us.

"Now, the trick is to take them carefully, so as not to break them, and sit them on your spoon like so," Mr. Jackdaw said, reaching over with chopsticks and delicately plucking out one of the dumplings. "It's hot, so let's give it some time. Please!"

I glanced at Mr. Scant, who hadn't moved, then back at Mr. Jackdaw. "I don't know how to use chopsticks," I said.

"Oh dear," said Mr. Jackdaw. "Wei, Tang, Lu, please be good chaps and help our guests."

Three of the big Chinese bodyguards pushed back their chairs, took our chopsticks, and reached out to the baskets in perfect unison. Each man plucked out a little dumpling, then gestured for us to pick up our spoons, leaning around us in a somewhat menacing way. Mr. Scant lifted his spoon, so I did too, and then Victor copied me, looking up at the bodyguard nearest to him apprehensively.

Once the men had placed dumplings on our spoons, Mr. Jackdaw said, "Splendid. Now we give it a few moments to cool down. And then comes the best part. You take a small bite from the bottom and drink the soup inside. Then, with that flavor rich in your mouth, you eat the rest. Like so."

During the whole process, his eyes flicked between me, Mr. Scant, and Victor. Not without some trepidation, imagining some lethal poison or, worse, the flavor of Brussels sprouts, I nibbled at my own dumpling. Soup immediately began to pour out, so I drank that first, then ate the rest. A rich flavor, not so different from a stew or particularly flavorsome broth, filled my mouth. The little treat was very agreeable.

Mr. Scant of course remained inscrutable while he ate, but Victor was nodding appreciatively. Mr. Jackdaw beamed at us, his thin face and straight teeth almost uncomfortably bright.

"There, wasn't that delicious?"

A long silence followed, which I felt I had better fill. "Yes, delicious," I conceded somewhat lamely.

Mr. Jackdaw went on grinning, then gave a little sideways gesture with his head. The men behind us returned to their seats, helping themselves to dumplings of their own. Victor said in French that he needed the toilet, so Mr. Jackdaw motioned to the big man next to him, the one who had not stood behind any of us, and the man nodded, then gestured for the little boy to get up. Victor looked to me in a panic.

"I'll go too," I said. I didn't really need to use the toilet myself, but I wasn't about to let these men take Victor out of my sight, even if they were supposed to be allies of Scotland Yard.

"Come back before the *bao* get cold, what?" Mr. Jackdaw said languidly.

The man escorting us toward a nearby door was shorter than Mr. Scant but very broad in the shoulders, with a beard that looked sharp at the edges and a shaven head with no queue. As we filed out, I looked back to Mr. Scant and heard him say, "Can we proceed directly to the part at which you tell us what you want from us?"

The water closet was grander than any I had seen, even in fine London hotels, and as richly decorated as the restaurant. We stepped toward one cubicle, and I balked at what looked like a hole in the ground, but Victor didn't seem perturbed in the least as he went inside. I went in the next cubicle and found, to my relief, that things looked much as I would have expected back in England, half a world away.

When we returned to the table, I was heartened to see Mr. Scant hadn't picked a fight with the other men.

". . . doing your work for you," Mr. Scant was saying.

"That's precisely my meaning—you are in a unique position," Mr. Jackdaw said. "I work for Scotland Yard. This is not a well-kept secret. If things go awry, I can be directly linked to Her Majesty. Which, rather fortuitously, you cannot be."

"You can't expect me to believe you don't have another plan," Mr. Scant said. "What if we had never come?"

"Of course there are other plans," Mr. Jackdaw replied. "They're simply not as feasible or efficient as this plan."

"What's happening?" I asked as I took my seat.

"I was just putting forward a proposition," said Mr. Jackdaw. "We think it is very agreeable. We will give you all the information on Miss Gaunt that we have—if you do something for us."

"Wait," I said. "If you have information on her, that means she's here, right? She must be in Shanghai."

Mr. Jackdaw's smile did not waver. "Perhaps. That's the kind of information you'll earn if you do as we ask, what?"

"But you wouldn't make us do something for you in Shanghai and then inform us that she's back in Europe, would you? So we must be on the right track." I grinned at Mr. Scant, feeling pleased with myself. "Isn't that right?"

Mr. Scant, staring down Mr. Jackdaw, didn't return my look. "Why should we trust you?"

"You trusted me in Paris, did you not?" Mr. Jackdaw asked. "Indeed, Paris is the reason we now trust *you*. We always keep our word in the Yard, and we're strong believers in healthy quid pro quo."

"What does he want us to do?" I asked Mr. Scant.

"Go and meet some criminals," said Mr. Scant. "And then do his spying work for him."

Mr. Jackdaw gave a raucous laugh, fully showing off those tombstone teeth of his, which all of a sudden seemed too big for his pointed face. "You certainly have a gift for turns of phrase, Scant. And a suspicious mind—that would be useful at the Yard. We're always in need of good men."

"You won't find one at this table."

"Now, now. The men back in England investigating the Ruminating Claw could always find new evidence, remember that. Evidence tying him to Diplexito Engineering, for example."

Mr. Scant's eyes narrowed. "Perhaps it would be better if only the boys and I left this place with our tongues."

"I'm used to threats," Mr. Jackdaw said. "Something I'm not used to is having to negotiate." He sat back and drank Chinese tea from his undersized cup. "You and I both know that if you say 'No,' your investigation ends there. You have no more leads, and we both know you're no Sherlock Holmes. You can walk away, but then you might as well go back to that funny little Beards and Binns dirigible of yours and begin the long journey home."

Mr. Scant pressed his lips together, saying nothing in response.

"Is it dangerous?" I asked.

"Potentially," said Mr. Jackdaw. "But I'm not asking just anyone."

"You will give us a place to stay and food to eat?" said Mr. Scant.

"You shall have precisely the food and lodgings I have. Very agreeable, I assure you."

"I don't feel we have much choice," said Mr. Scant. "I'll do it."

Mr. Jackdaw gave me a bad feeling. He had seemed very charming when we first met him in France, but he had a head that appeared to have too much skin on it, too much confidence, and a smile that never reached his eyes. He looked as though he was wearing someone else's face and putting on a slightly exaggerated act to match their personality.

He and his men took us to the Bund, which is where I realized that Shanghai was a city just as modern and busy as London or Paris. The Bund was a wide road on the side of a river that was broader than any I had ever seen before. There were no pagodas or temples to be seen but rather large modern buildings and a big iron bridge. I had the uncanny feeling of having returned to Europe somehow, and on the streets, a number of Europeans tipped their hats to us as we passed. Mr. Jackdaw greeted many of them as though they were close friends, though I was unsure if it was all an act.

We were led into a newly built clubhouse with lodgings, rather like a particularly grand London gentlemen's club, and shown to our accomodations. There was a convenient partitioned room available, so that Mr. Scant could sleep in one bed, I could sleep in another, and a suitable cot could be brought in for Victor. With grudging thanks to Mr. Jackdaw, we put what belongings we had carried with us into the room, and I decided to take off my jacket. I dropped it on the bed, along with Mr. Jackdaw's chocolate eggs, and noticed Victor was doing the same. Mr. Scant showed no sign of discomfort in his long jacket, though Shanghai's weather was much warmer than London's.

Later that evening, Mr. Jackdaw held a "briefing" in the bar of the clubhouse, a bar he boasted was the longest in the world. He spoke so proudly that I wondered if he thought he had carved it himself. He sat with us at a table across from the great mahogany expanse, cradling a gin and tonic that I was sure he had ordered only for the look of the thing, while an old Chinese man quietly swept the floor just beyond the bar's single bend.

"You're to meet one Mr. Yau," Mr. Jackdaw told Mr. Scant. "He speaks perfect English, of course. Studied in Hong Kong—a lot of these secret society troublemaker types did. You've had experience with secret societies, I know—a lot of talk about magic and overthrowing their governments. The ones here are rather more likely to do the latter than our home-grown specimens. In fact, there was an attempt at a revolutionary uprising outside Hong Kong just a month or two back. Beastly business."

"Are the people that unhappy?" I asked.

"You remember your teacher's lecture, don't you?" said Mr. Jackdaw, with a smirk at Mr. Scant.

"This whole country's a kettle left on the fire too long. It's already boiling over, and that just makes the fire jump up underneath it all the more, what? And into the middle of it all you come a-wading. A curious happenstance."

"There is nothing curious about it," Mr. Scant said in a dull tone. "You know why we're here. I have no doubt this unrest is what pulled my niece to this country, in whatever capacity she is operating. We have simply followed her."

"Hmm!" Mr. Jackdaw grinned again. "You've had a long history of being drawn to dangerous places by *happenstance*, haven't you? But now that you're here, let's be kind to one other, what? I think that's in everybody's best interests."

"So what am I hoping to achieve for you?" asked Mr. Scant.

"Mr. Yau works for the Star and Stone Association, a nationwide crime syndicate. They are procuring weapons manufactured in Europe, and your job is to pose as the contact from the manufacturers, then find out what they intend to do with the arms once they have them. There is a festival later this week, one the Xuantong Emperor himself is scheduled to attend, so we need to know what to expect."

"When is this meeting scheduled?" Mr. Scant asked.

Mr. Jackdaw smiled. "You arrived at the perfect time. It's tomorrow morning."

And so we returned, feeling a little dazed, to the rooms Mr. Jackdaw had arranged for us. Of course, Victor wanted to know what we were doing to find his brother, and whatever assurances Mr. Scant gave him, the rest of that evening was spent watching him closely to make sure he didn't go out into the streets of Shanghai looking for Julien.

The next morning, Mr. Jackdaw used the telephones in our rooms to wake us. After we were washed and dressed, he met us in the entrance lobby with his usual charming yet insincere grin. "Are we ready for the day's adventure?" he said, but we had no answer for him.

"I want to go with Mr. Scant," I said.

"Out of the question, I'm afraid," said Mr. Jackdaw. "They are expecting one older gentleman, and one older gentleman only."

He led us to the large iron bridge nearby and then gestured to a little service door on the far bank. "That's the place."

Mr. Scant handed me his claw for safekeeping

as we crossed the bridge. Mr. Jackdaw, Victor, and I stopped halfway to watch him use the secret knock Mr. Jackdaw had shown him on the bridge's service door. Mr. Scant had to speak a password before the door opened, and then he was swallowed by darkness. Victor and I were left on the bridge with Mr. Jackdaw, who smiled at us again.

"This heat is beastly," he said, "and your valet is going to be some time. They like to put on a show of their power, these *hongmen*. Let's go and find some English tea."

As we walked, Mr. Jackdaw explained that *hongmen* were members of a secret society who had proven their worth to their fellows. Victor, uninterested in this English chatter, went to ask him again about his brother Julien, and not only did Mr. Jackdaw give reassurances that seemed to lift the boy's spirits, he offered his hand. Mr. Jackdaw walked with the boy like a father with his son, which only made me narrow my eyes in suspicion. The man gave me the feeling of being doused in some unpleasant oil and ending up coated so thoroughly I had no way to wipe myself clean. I loosened my collar.

Mr. Jackdaw had made it sound as though we would search for a teahouse, but in fact he led us to a nearby hotel—less grand than the clubhouse where we had our lodgings, but nonetheless very luxurious. On an upper floor was an opulent dining room, entirely bereft of anything Chinese. Sitting there, we could have been sitting in Claridge's or the Ritz. Taking a place at the central table under a frozen firework of pretty yellow flowers, Mr. Jackdaw ordered afternoon tea.

"It's like we're not in China at all anymore," I said to Mr. Jackdaw.

"I know, isn't it marvelous?"

I frowned. "I thought you liked the local food."

"I do. But more than that, what I like is the culture that exists at this exact moment. I admire it for its fragility, like, ah . . . like the moment the mayfly spreads its wings to the only sunset it will ever see." He chuckled to himself. "A snowflake that melts on the fingertip. Just now, Shanghai is a beautiful collision of two cultures, each one thinking it is superior to the other. Here in the Bund, along its great river, the Europeans want to rebuild Europe, and the Americans are only too happy to help. Meanwhile, walk for ten minutes that-a-way and you'll come to the Old City, or 'Chinatown,' as these Europeans have the presumptuousness to call it. Ah, thank you."

The waiter, young and fair-haired and well-turned-out, had arrived with a tray. He laid out a pretty tea service patterned in pink and gold, and a three-tiered tea stack replete with neatly cut sandwiches, dainty tarts, and colorful French macaroons. Victor's hands went straight for a vanilla macaroon, but Mr. Jackdaw swatted it away, and then pointed at the sandwiches. Victor seemed amused rather than upset and took a cucumber sandwich instead.

"When you go to the Old City, the true city," Mr. Jackdaw continued, "out of this pretty shell, you'll see real life and a real culture. Beggars, cripples, and worse than all besides, Marxists. The Europeans all sneer at the poor here and look at them like animals, forgetting the destitute in every city and town in their own countries. So here there are two separate worlds. Are you following me?"

"I think so," I said.

"Smart lad. Europe, especially our own dear motherland, has spent the last hundred, two hundred years ensuring that this country *needs* us. We can't let China hoard all its riches to itself, can we? So we did terrible things to the people here. Yet even now, the Chinese continue to play the game we invited them to, and smile as they do it, because in today's modern world, you can't just shut the rest of the world out."

I finished my ham sandwich and moved on to a fruit tart. Victor took some too and surprised me by asking, in English, "Is there custard?"

"No custard," I said. "But there is some clotted cream."

"No custard," Victor repeated sadly, but he reached for the cream nonetheless.

I looked back to Mr. Jackdaw. I had been concentrating hard, trying to follow what he said. "So I suppose China is doing the right thing by dealing with all the other countries. If you can't shut the world out anyway."

Mr. Jackdaw was enjoying a scone in the style of cream tea. "Hmm, difficult to say. China did some clever things. It gave us foreigners these ports to play in, to build our hotels and our churches and our gentlemen's clubs so we can pretend we're at home. Like the little slice of England we sit in today.

"Now, for the most part, we stay in these little cities and don't cause trouble. And when the Empress Dowager found herself on the wrong side of the Boxer Rebellion, she escaped from Peking and hid herself away deep in the heart of the country. Sensible to keep that division, I think. Nevertheless: defeat after defeat, in an age of empires and conquest—the country looks weak. Today, the Empress Dowager is gone, and on the throne is a small boy. And that's where Shanghai becomes a snowflake."

I paused with a macaroon halfway to my mouth. "Another country is going to take over?"

"No. The keg of gunpowder lying under all this is Chinese pride. The Xuantong Emperor and his handlers bow to foreign powers while the men toil in the fields and factories, all so that debts from old wars can be paid. What do you think happens next, young Master Diplexito?"

"Well, you said they were proud . . ."

"And so?"

"They fight the foreigners?"

"They tried that and failed. So what other choice is there? If the people can't fight the foreigners, who else do they hold responsible for this mess?"

"They have a revolution, like Mr. Scant says."

Mr. Jackdaw smiled. "And as far as we can, we at the Yard want to stop that happening. Now why don't you and I go and look at the view?"

As the dining room was on an upper floor, the windows afforded pleasant views of the surrounding city. I could see the bridge where Mr. Scant was meeting the mysterious criminals, and then beyond the river, the gradual change of the city from large Western-style buildings to small and intricate wooden ones—the start of the Old City that Mr. Jackdaw had mentioned.

Mr. Jackdaw spoke again. "Last year, you fought against a society that wanted to control a government from the shadows. Here, those same societies mean to *become* the government. Can you imagine that in England? Well, that's what you and your dear tutor have stepped into."

"We just want to find Mr. Scant's niece. But thank you for explaining things. You know an awful lot about all this."

Mr. Jackdaw's smile was almost bashful, but as artificial as ever. "It is rather my job, you know. And whether in France or Zanzibar or China, I'm still just reading different chapters of the same story. I abhor chaos, but at this stage, I don't think it can be avoided. So our interest now is in ensuring that whatever happens, however this country changes, Britain does not become China's enemy."

"I don't want that either."

Mr. Jackdaw smiled. "So what *do* you want, young Master Diplexito?"

"It's all very complicated. But I feel bad that China has been bullied for so long. I want them to be able to stand up for themselves."

"That's a good way to put it," Mr. Jackdaw said. "But for my part, I feel rather as though the playground bullies don't realize that they're kicking not a helpless schoolmate but rather a sleeping bear."

"I'd like to hear from some Chinese people about it."

"It's refreshing to hear that. Here, most of us insulate ourselves against the local language and culture."

"Is Mr. Scant safe?"

"Safe? Oh no, none of us is safe." He took a deep bite of his scone and chewed thoughtfully. "But one thing I can tell you for certain, you're both much safer here than you were in France."

IX
A Pursuit

Scant's face was as dour and inscrutable as ever as he climbed the stairs to meet us. "Let's keep walking," he rumbled when he was close enough for us to hear. We walked over the large iron bridge, where the wind from the sea scythed and whistled above us. Here, he decided to stop and look out to the water, as Mr. Jackdaw simply stood aside, grinning his strange grin. After a time, Mr. Scant spoke.

"The long and short of it is that the Star and Stone Association has a special deposit in the Peking-Shanghai Bank that only a 'white ghost' can withdraw, going through a special contact."

"And you got the name of this contact?" said Mr. Jackdaw.

"Not a name, only a rather lifelike sketch," said

Mr. Scant. "I don't see the harm in showing you."

He produced a drawing of a mousy-faced older man who looked more like a geography teacher than a criminal, though I supposed if you could tell at a glance someone was a criminal they wouldn't be very good at the job. Mr. Jackdaw nodded, still grinning, but said nothing.

"We've been given a time and place to find him tomorrow," said Mr. Scant. "I would prefer that we leave it to you, but they took great pains drawing my likeness too, so I assume I have to do this as well."

"We'd very much appreciate it," said Mr. Jackdaw. "I'll give you everything you need over dinner."

"This is going beyond what we bargained for."

"If only you'd manipulated them into not using your likeness . . ." said Mr. Jackdaw, with a sad smile this time.

"What actually happened in there?" I asked.

"As Mr. Jackdaw explained, the Star and Stone Association is not so very different from our own dear Woodhouselee Society. Its members call themselves shadow rulers and used theatrics to leave an impression on me. Smoke and costumes and strange muffled sounds. But under it all, the thing that matters most to them is money. They told me they would use these weapons to steal from the banks here in the city, to better fund the wider revolution. But that may have just been the impression they wanted to give to Mr. Welles."

"Who is Mr. Welles?" I asked.

"The man I was impersonating, who I assume Scotland Yard has somehow arranged not to be anywhere near Shanghai just now."

Mr. Jackdaw didn't reply to that, but instead said, "I'll brief you again about tomorrow before I take my leave this evening."

"Take your leave?" I said. "Are you going somewhere? What about the meeting with the man at the bank?"

"Alas, I can only ask that you do this for me and support you from afar. Recall that the Yard must not be involved in any way. And I do have a number of other tasks I must see to, but I will not be far away, and of course I need to give you the information you seek." When nobody had any answer for him, he grinned again, held out his arms, and said, "For dinner, I think some Hong Kong–style dim sum."

Hong Kong–style dim sum turned out to be small savory dishes, served hot in the same baskets as the *xiao long bao*. Mr. Jackdaw picked out mysterious-sounding foods from trolleys pushed around the restaurant by smiling waitresses. Unlike the other establishments Mr. Jackdaw had taken us to, this one was busy, every table occupied by Chinese patrons. One even raised his cup of tea to me when I met his eye, smiling warmly in a way that deepened the wrinkles all about his friendly face, wrinkles all in entirely different places from Mr. Scant's. I raised my teacup in return and tried one of the dumplings, which was delicious.

Mr. Scant now regarded Mr. Jackdaw with constant suspicion, and Mr. Jackdaw clearly enjoyed that fact. When Mr. Scant asked when his side of the bargain would be considered completed, Mr. Jackdaw raised a finger as though to admonish him.

"Tomorrow will be the end of it," he said. "Do believe me, if this goes badly, I'm the one who's in the most trouble."

"I wonder about that," said Mr. Scant.

After enjoying a few particularly fluffy white buns filled with sweetened meat, Victor pulled my sleeve and pointed to the old lady who owned the restaurant, who had waved at him and gestured for him to come over. While Mr. Scant and Mr. Jackdaw discussed how to find the place where Mr.

Scant would meet the bank contact tomorrow, Victor dragged me over. Although he and the restaurant owner each spoke in their own language, without a shred of shared comprehension, somehow Victor managed to exchange his Indian cap for a kind of pointed Chinese hat with a black sheet hanging down from the back, like a small cloak. It was too big for him, but he put it on his head undeterred.

After the meal, Mr. Jackdaw bade us goodnight with a rather exaggerated bow, and we withdrew to our rooms in the clubhouse. As Mr. Scant helped me prepare for bed, Victor stood squarely in front of me.

"Where is Julien?" he asked. He was picking up English quickly, but I wasn't sure he could understand my answers.

"We don't know," I said, slowly. "Tomorrow, we look for a man. Then we find a girl. Hopefully she will know about it."

"I want Julien."

I corrected him—"'I want to *find* Julien'"—but he went over to his bed to flop onto it. I wasn't sure if he was only pretending to cry, but after seeing him lying there in my old clothes, I looked back at Mr. Scant.

"Do we *know* his brother is here?"

"No," said Mr. Scant. "He says he overheard men saying that's where young men would be taken, and it would be quite the coincidence if there is no connection. But certainly this trip could end without us ever finding the lad."

"What would we do then?"

"I don't know," said Mr. Scant. "Some lessons in life are truly hard."

Victor was soon asleep, so I took off his outer clothes and put him into the bed, then settled down to read the book about Chinese history Mr. Scant had read before me. Though the exploits of great Chinese explorer Cheng Ho were fairly gripping, my eyes grew heavy as I read, and when I had to check if he had really given a giraffe to the emperor as a gift or if I had dreamed it, I decided it was time to sleep.

The next day, Mr. Scant woke us late. We ate breakfast in the French style in the clubhouse restaurant, and I said to Victor that he must be happy to see French food, but he frowned at his croissant. "This is French?" he asked, in English, and I realized he had probably eaten very few buffet breakfasts in his life.

Mr. Jackdaw had left a map for us to follow. Our destination was a little way into the Old City, through the rather ramshackle city walls. From above, I had seen how the city changed from one thing to another over a surprisingly short distance, but walking into the Old City, I realized the difference was far greater than shifts in the styles of the buildings. The people, the sounds, the smells, the very air itself all seemed different as we walked into the Shanghai its own people had built.

We passed some very beautiful buildings with perfect miniature gardens, as well as a temple the size of a village church. A large burner outside the temple exhaled fragrant incense, like a steam train with all but its chimney buried in the ground. At the same time, not everything in the old city was beautiful. The straw underfoot was sodden, we passed more than one dead animal that I tried to prevent Victor from seeing, and many of the denizens we passed plucked and pinched at us and had to be driven away by Mr. Scant. I positioned Victor in front of me and held on to his shoulders, while Mr. Scant stood very close, looking this way and that warily.

"Oh!" I said, as our destination came into view.

"The Willow Pattern Tea House," said Mr. Scant.

At home, Mother had some chinaware with the famous Blue Willow pattern on it, and before us was a grand old edifice that looked rather like one of the buildings from that design. It stood two stories high, topped by pretty roofs that resembled the heads of immense flowers. Each corner of the eaves rose up like arms held high in exultation, and the walls were carved in intricate patterns. White paper covered the windows, as though the whole building were a great floating lantern. Indeed, as if to enhance this impression, the whole structure stood on stilts in a little lake, with a zigzag bridge stretching out to meet it. This probably would have given a more pleasant impression had the water not looked and smelled like a swamp, with various unsavory things floating in it.

"Is it really the place from the Blue Willow pattern?" I asked.

"I'm told that the local guides will say it is," Mr. Scant said, "but in truth, it only bears a pleasant resemblance. Shall we go?"

The bridge was pretty to regard, but at each corner sat a beggar, holding up palms or bowls, speaking words I could not understand. One particularly sad-looking girl of about my age could only whisper at me, and I wished I had some of the local coins to give her. I recalled the bonbons from Mr. Jackdaw that I had meant to give to Victor, and deciding the girl's need was greater than mine or his just now, I gave them to her. She looked delighted for a moment, before she was beset by the others on the bridge and took to her feet to scramble away. I was not sure the chocolates would be entirely good for her, but they would fill her belly, and perhaps she could exchange some for better food. Victor watched her go indifferently, then looked up to me and said, "Maybe friend." I remembered our first meeting had been very similar.

Inside the tea shop, the mood was very different. A little old Chinese man, who looked like he too had been carved from wood, came to greet us. "Welcome, welcome," he said with a thick accent, then pointed delightedly at Victor's hat. "A scholar! Very good! Come sit. Tea? Tea."

"Yes, please," said Mr. Scant. I could only assume he had been given some of the local money by Mr. Jackdaw or had it exchanged at the clubhouse. The interior of the teahouse matched the exterior, with numerous little wooden stools and square tables carved into the angular shapes so popular in China. Most of the numerous patrons were Chinese, their clothes neat and clean, all of them with their hair in queues or under tight round caps, but three or four groups included Westerners. I heard English spoken in strange accents I had never heard before, and wondered if I might be hearing an Australian or Canadian or even a South African for the first time.

Tea was served by a bored-looking young woman, and though Mr. Scant poured it, the steam suggested it was much too hot to drink, so he did not distribute the little squat teacups. All the while, he was looking around the room.

"Is he here?" I said. "The man from the drawing?"

"He's here," said Mr. Scant, busying himself with the cups.

The teahouse was a noisy place. The table next to us had noticed Victor's hat as well and found it very amusing, waving to him repeatedly. He enjoyed the attention and waved back. "Good hat," he remarked to me, and put his chin on the table happily.

When the tea was cool enough to drink, I did not find it a particular delight. It had been served without milk or sugar and tasted rather like the water that sometimes got in your mouth after a particularly vicious rugby tackle. The old man brought over little baked tarts of some sort, served with jam, and presented them to Victor, saying, "For scholar! No charge!" He waited for Victor to try the treat and shuffled away contentedly when Victor grinned.

"Custard is . . . the good," said Victor, as he offered the rest of the treats to Mr. Scant and me. "Most good."

"The *best*," I said, and tried the little tart.

"Oh my," said Mr. Scant, chewing his portion. "Very sweet."

"I like sweet things," I said. "I think you're the only one here who doesn't."

"'Sweet' I can tolerate," said Mr. Scant. "But I think I have lost all feeling in my mouth." He took a sip of tea and swilled it about. I laughed, and so did Victor.

I wasn't sure how he did it, but Mr. Scant had been watching his charge so closely that he ordered our bill a mere moment before the same request was called by another table. Mr. Scant paid in coins, which I had read were called *tael*, and we stepped out into the warm early-summer's day just as the party of English and Chinese men behind us were settling their bill. If anything, it would have looked as though they were following us. I tried to surreptitiously look for the mouse-faced man from the sketch, but Mr. Scant did not even glance behind us. Victor got a pat on his scholar's hat from the owner as we left, which pushed it over his eyes, and he pantomimed being blind. Playing along, I could look back quite naturally as we again traversed the zigzag bridge. At the end, Mr. Scant led us off in the direction of the river.

"Don't we need to be *behind* him to follow him?" I asked.

"Walking ahead is a much better way not to arouse suspicion."

Our walk back toward the Bund took us past a large racing track, which I thought was a park until I saw the enormous grandstand. Only a few yards behind us, some of the men said their good-byes and left the group there, but we didn't pause. We simply walked on without waiting, and I had to trust Mr. Scant had ensured the mousey man was not one of those who had left the group. Finally, we came to the river. Victor was complaining of the heat by then, so we stopped for a time and went to buy shaved ice with berries from a nearby vendor. Pausing to eat that, we let the man and his remaining companions pass, and then continued after them. I caught sight of him for the first time, with his rounded cheeks and pointed nose.

We kept a cautious distance until the man was

alone, which happened while he was on the Bund, near a big clock tower with plentiful gothic ornamentation. As we pressed closer, I made a point of staying close to Mr. Scant, grateful that Victor, energized by his shaved ice, made no complaint when we increased our pace.

"Should we catch him?" I asked.

Mr. Scant nodded and pulled down his hat a little before breaking into a short run. He cleared his throat as he approached the man.

"Mr. Adams?"

The little man turned to look at Mr. Scant and frowned suspiciously. "Yes?"

"My name is Richard Welles. Do you have a moment?"

"I'm in a bit of a hurry. My manager doesn't take kindly to us being even five seconds late."

"It won't take a moment." He produced a letter. "I'm told you will understand if you read this."

The man hesitated but then took the letter and looked at the seal. Seeming to recognize it, he opened the letter, then looked at Mr. Scant with renewed interest. "An esteemed customer indeed, Mr. Welles. Please, come with me. Ah, these are your children? Let's go together."

He led us into the large bank, nodding at two large guards, all the while chattering brightly at Mr. Scant. "It's rare to welcome one of our exclusive customers, a splendid treat and no mistaking." He turned to a young clerk and, without stopping, said, "Please tell Mr. Linden that I have upper-tier guests and I'll be at the meeting just as soon as we're finished." He grinned back at Mr. Scant again. "As we promised when the deposit was made, our security is the finest in the world and constantly improving. You have your key and pass phrase, I presume?"

Mr. Scant nodded, patting his jacket demonstratively.

"Splendid, splendid. Please step into the elevator."

Once we were inside and the doors were pulled closed, Mr. Adams looked at us with the twinkling eyes of a toymaker showing off his latest creation. He put a key into a small hole under the elevator buttons, and the elevator shuddered into operation, going down. After some time, it stopped, and Mr. Adams opened the doors again, letting in air so chilly that we had clearly traveled deep underground.

Ahead of us was a large safe. A big, bearded security guard stood beside it, but judging by the stool behind him, he had been sitting until we appeared.

"A happy day, Jeffreys!" Mr. Adams said to the guard. "A customer has come to retrieve his deposit. Open the vault!"

The big man nodded, and after Mr. Adams went forward to enter his combination, the guard turned the big wheel that opened the door. I wondered if this was all for show—until the large door swung open and I saw just how thick the metal was. On the other side of the doorway were a number of smaller locked safes and cabinets.

"I'm afraid you are not permitted to step inside," Mr. Adams said to Mr. Scant. "May I have your pass phrase?"

Mr. Scant licked his lips and then carefully said, "Know thine enemy and know thyself: win a hundred battles without danger."

Mr. Adams nodded and held out his hand, into which Mr. Scant put a golden key. I wasn't sure whether he had procured this from the Star and Stone Association or from Mr. Jackdaw. Then Mr. Adams turned to go inside the vault, while Mr. Jeffreys, the guard, stood blocking our way. After a time, Mr. Adams came out holding a box, a look of excitement on his face. "Let's go back upstairs to finish the paperwork," he said. "To tell the truth, I mostly wanted to show the little ones the vault entrance. Rather exciting, don't you think?"

"It was," I agreed.

Upstairs, we went to a counter in the main room of the bank, and Mr. Scant was instructed to sign several pieces of paper. Then, finally, Mr. Adams turned the box toward us and opened it with a flourish, saying, "Voilà!"

I caught a glimpse of a golden statue of some sort in the box, but pink smoke immediately started to pour from the box into the room. Mr. Scant and I both reacted without hesitation, slamming the box shut together, but I drew my hand back just as quickly, because the box was hot enough to scald. The smoke began to force its way out from between the cracks, some of it now black as well as pink, and Mr. Adams went into a panic. "What is this? What is this?" he kept saying.

When the box burst into flames, more cries of surprise rang throughout the bank, and somebody set off an alarm. "Out! Everybody out!" Mr. Adams cried.

Mr. Scant pulled me and Victor toward the exit, but a crowd of people all trying to get through had created a blockage at the door, so for a time we were stuck in the room as the pink gas filled it. I held my handkerchief to my mouth and pulled Victor's out, showing him how to do the same. Looking back at the burning box, I watched as some of the wood fell away, revealing a golden dragon inside, with red eyes that seemed to stare directly at me.

Once we were outside, Mr. Scant swept us away from the group gathering outside the building and into a nearby passageway.

"What happened?" I asked.

"We were set up."

"Set up for what? Is it a bomb?"

"I don't know. I don't see what this achieved. Sheer idiocy."

Mr. Scant led us around a few buildings and then back to the road, where we called over a cab. Its cabin only provided for two people, but we squeezed in. The driver didn't speak English, so Mr. Scant showed him the business card for the Shanghai Club, the site of our lodgings. The driver nodded, and we were in motion.

"What do we do now?" I asked.

"We ask Jackdaw what he was playing at."

"What was that smoke? Was it dangerous?"

"Just a kind of flare smoke, I think," Mr. Scant said. "Nothing harmful. But I can't be sure. We can only be certain that someone wanted to send a message."

Back at the Shanghai Club, Mr. Jackdaw was waiting in the bar, a copy of the *Times* and a gin and tonic at his side. The way Mr. Scant marched up to him, I thought a fight was about to erupt. Mr. Jackdaw's smile wavered just a little. "Something's wrong," he said, peering at Mr. Scant over his reading glasses.

"Yes, something's wrong," Mr. Scant snapped. "This was a setup. There was no package for Mr. Richard Welles, only a smoke bomb to be set off in the middle of the bank."

"What? Why?"

"You tell us. I assume the Star and Stone Association wanted to show the foreign banks it can get to them at any time it pleases."

Mr. Jackdaw folded the paper neatly and placed it down, then took off his glasses. "Was there an explosion?"

"It was just a smoke bomb," said Mr. Scant. "To cause panic. I'm sure it will be in all the newspapers."

"It most certainly will not," Mr. Jackdaw replied. "I'll see to that. But do you mean to say that for however many years, at no doubt a great expense to the organization, the Star and Stone has stored a smoke bomb inside the bank vault, just to cause a bit of harmless panic when it goes off? There are so many ways to make a political point. Something else must be afoot here."

"That man Adams will know my face."

"I'll look for him," Mr. Jackdaw said distractedly. "This is very peculiar. I need to talk to my *hongmen* contact. I don't mind telling you, I'm vexed. Quite, quite vexed. But even so, a deal's a deal. Here's what you wanted."

Mr. Jackdaw handed over another of the club-house's business cards, on which someone had scrawled a number of Chinese characters.

"Is it an address?" I asked.

"More or less," said Mr. Jackdaw. "Show this to a cab driver or a rickshaw man. He'll take you where you need to go to find out about your niece. And now, I have a mess to sort out. Excuse me."

He pushed his hat onto his head, but I interrupted him. "Mr. Jackdaw, one moment?"

"One and only one," Mr. Jackdaw said sharply.

"What about Victor's brother? Is he here?"

Mr. Jackdaw gave a little nod. "I can't give a full confirmation because names haven't been recorded, but the Yard understands that the Star and Stone Association has brought a number of young Frenchmen to the city. I don't know where they're kept, but it's likely the boy is with the rest."

There was no time to rest. Victor asked Mr. Scant whether we were going to find Julien, and to the best of my understanding, Mr. Scant told him that we were going to find the people who might know where Julien was. By the time we were outside again, we were almost running.

After showing the address to the first driver we hailed, the man looked at us as though we were insane and drove away. The second laughed. The third appeared incredulous but called over a rickshaw driver, who shrugged and held out his palm for payment.

When we were crammed into the man's little conveyance, he said, "Okay, here we go," and set off at a remarkable pace. The ride was bumpy, but the man seemed to be enjoying hauling us along, often laughing or shouting at someone he passed, even jumping in the air once or twice. We passed what must have been the cathedral Mr. Jackdaw mentioned, two tall proud steeples stretching up into the sky like red bishops from some immense chessboard. The rickshaw rolled on until finally our driver stopped in a crowded and unremarkable city street, waited until we alighted, then crowed out, "Bye-bye now!" and disappeared.

Men walked past, talking in French, and Victor's eyes widened. He shifted his feet as though to chase after them, but then he heard another voice and realized all the Europeans around us were speaking his language. Delighted, he greeted a young couple, and they happily exchanged pleasantries with him. Mr. Scant went to join them and showed them the characters on the card, but they shrugged, clearly unable to read what it said.

"Hu Bao," I said. "*La nom est* Hu Bao." I couldn't remember whether *la nom* or *le nom* was right for *the name*, but I knew they would understand either way. And they clearly did, because their expressions darkened. The man pointed at a shop a few doors down, then pulled down his hat a little, while the woman covered her mouth and whispered to him as they hurried away. Undeterred, Mr. Scant led us to the door the man had indicated.

Once inside, we were met with silence, the silence of a room full of people who had stopped talking to stare at the newcomers who had walked in through the doors.

The room was smoky enough that you could tell the cigarette smell would linger long after the people had cleared out. Customers sat shoulder to shoulder around hexagonal tables, dressed in unremarkable Chinese clothes in various shades of green. Every man in the room was wearing green, in fact, or brown with small green accents. Their teapots bore green patterns, and I could see that even the dice some of the men were rolling on the table had green detailing. None of the men wore a queue—all had their hair shaved very close to their heads, like the images of Buddhist monks I had seen, only the men here bore scars and false eyes instead of serene expressions of peace.

One particularly tall and fearsome-looking man, with a face that looked as though it had been made with a bare minimum of skin to cover the skull beneath, stood up. "*Oui?*" he said.

Emboldened by hearing his mother tongue, Victor couldn't help himself. "*Mon frère Julien est—*"

Unfortunately, Victor had decided to step forward as he spoke about his brother, and the reaction had been instant and terrifying. Men jumped up at once, pulling out knives and pistols and even a curved sword or two. Someone had stepped forward to grab Victor, but Mr. Scant rushed forward to grab the man's wrist, and then another two men advanced on Mr. Scant with blades drawn. With a deft movement across his hip, Mr. Scant brought his free hand up with the claw in place, raised to deflect the knives if they came too close. That was when everything exploded into a blur of motion and I felt myself grabbed from behind, strong arms seizing me around my chest.

"Stop!" I yelled, but it made no difference. "Let go of me! Let go of me!"

But someone else had their arm around my neck now. Mr. Scant was coming my way, but too many blades had appeared in his path, so I took the deepest breath I could and shouted the one thing I thought could help us. *"Cai Zhao-Ji!"*

From deep in the room, another voice pierced the noise, and the tall man shouted in turn. All weapons were sheathed and hidden back under clothes and tables, and everyone was seated again. Everyone except for the tall man and, in a dark corner of the room, a small group of young people, two men and two women. The men I did not know, but the women I had seen before. One was the only other Westerner in the tearoom, the girl we had searched around the world for: Uncle Reggie's daughter, Elspeth Gaunt.

The other was her partner and our savior, Miss Cai Zhao-Ji, who was now stepping forward. For a time, the only sounds were her footsteps and Victor's soft whining.

"You're here at last," Cai Zhao-Ji said when she was upon us. "And just as I've come to expect from Englishmen, you've brought a big mess with you."

X

The Viridian Clan

"T"he day after tomorrow is Duanwu, the festival of the dragon boats," said Cai Zhao-Ji. "The Xuantong Emperor himself will be in the city. That's when we expect the Star and Stone to make its move."

"Mr. Jackdaw mentioned something about that," I said. There weren't enough seats at the table in the corner, so we stood awkwardly around the place where the small group had been sitting. The men, who had not yet introduced themselves, were regarding us with suspicion. They resembled university students, wearing Western suits and neckties despite the heat, and while they wore their hair short, it was not shaved close to their heads.

Mr. Scant was uninterested. "With all due respect, Master Oliver, we've found what we were looking for. Elspeth, please come back to England with us. Your father is waiting and took a terrible beating searching for you in Paris."

"I haven't finished my tea," Elspeth said. "Nor have I finished my business in China. I'll write Father a letter. I didn't want to worry him by writing from Shanghai, but it seems he is worried anyway."

Miss Cai seemed to remember something. "Ah, speaking of letters, did you not get mine when you were in Paris? It would have told you what was happening here, without your having to come. I sent it with a man I trust. He should have brought it to you at any cost."

"No letter," Mr. Scant said.

"That's a worry."

Mr. Scant shook his head. "In any event, we find ourselves in this situation, and the most important thing for me is to get you, Elspeth, back home to your father."

"Father sent me away under the care of a criminal organization when I was seven years old," said Miss Gaunt. "He can wait until my business in China is finished. I'll write to him."

"I'm afraid I really must insist."

One of the men in Western suits spoke for the

first time. "What makes you think you're in any position to insist?"

"Ah, we haven't done introductions," said Miss Cai. "Deng, Song, as you know, this is Mr. Scant, Master Diplexito, and Master Veyron. The older boy and his valet helped us with the Woodhouselee business in England. Mr. Scant, Master Diplexito, Master Veyron, may I present Deng Shu-Ming and Song Yu-Sheng?"

The men bowed from where they sat, so I did the same, and chorused "Very nice to meet you," along with everyone else—including Victor. But something had struck me. "Master Veyron?" I said, as realization struck. "That's Victor's surname? I never thought to ask . . ."

"How amusing," said Miss Gaunt.

"But how did you know it?" I asked.

"We have our networks," said Miss Cai.

"Does that mean you know about his brother? Is he here?"

"Not here," said Miss Cai. "But close." She had a clever face, with thin lips that were always twitching with amusement and bright dark eyes that darted from place to place as though calculating how to disassemble and reassemble everything she saw. She was in many ways opposite to Miss Gaunt, whose every movement seemed languid and simple, as though calculated in advance to be as effortless as possible. Elspeth Gaunt had her uncle's piercing gray-green eyes and thoughtful brow, albeit without his bushy eyebrows, and her mouth was always turned down as if in disappointment with the world.

"I do hope we can find the boy's brother," said Mr. Scant, "but I made a promise that I would return my niece safely to England. That is my priority."

"Your niece can decide for herself where she goes," said Miss Gaunt, fixing her uncle with a stare that he returned. When their eyes met, I felt as though the room's temperature dropped several degrees.

"Uncle Reggie *is* very worried about you," I said in what I hoped was a placatory tone. "We can work everything out about debts, and I promise you he's sorry for everything that happened because of the Society."

Miss Gaunt broke eye contact with Mr. Scant to look at me. "Neither of you understands my situation at all. Father's debt hasn't mattered for months. The owner of this teahouse, our leader here, took on the debt for my sake, and I have worked to repay it, very nearly in full. I wanted my father to pay his own debts, but that became impossible to arrange. What matters is that I'm part of something important now."

She let those words hang in the air. "Well said," murmured one of the young men, Mr. Song, as he raised his cigarette to his lips. The two men, Deng and Song, looked similar to one another, though not similar enough to be brothers. They were both handsome young fellows, with determined faces and serious expressions, confident in their own strength and intelligence. Mr. Deng was slightly broader in the shoulders than Mr. Song, with a wider jaw and wider nose, while Mr. Song's eyes were set farther apart.

"This something, is it . . . some sort of international police?" I chanced, remembering what Mr. Scant had said in London. The reaction from the two men was sudden and fierce.

"Who told you that?" barked Mr. Deng. "What are your sources?"

"Relax," said Miss Cai. "After Elspeth and I intervened in England, it would not have been hard for Oliver or his valet to figure out the rest." She let out a little sigh as the two men settled down, and then looked at me very seriously.

"In Shanghai, there are three secret societies. The largest is the Star and Stone Association—a group that's spread all over the country but is most visible here. Its members have a lot of money and influence, and mean to overthrow the emperor. Then there is the Tri-Loom, which is serious about being a secret society. We know of a few members, but the Tri-Loom operates in the shadows, without a leader or a headquarters. And then there is the Viridian Clan, based in the Hu Bao Tea House, where we now sit. Not everything the Viridian Clan has done in its long history has been exactly noble, or indeed legal, but the leader has bright ideas for the future. He's a man you should meet. In fact, you will meet him now, having come into his teahouse and drunk his tea. Leaving without paying your respects would be a great insult."

"Lucky for you, he's my father," said Mr. Song. "I'll make the introductions."

"And you?" Miss Cai pointed her finger very rudely at Mr. Scant. "You keep your mouth shut."

Behind the tearoom lay a little alleyway that had been blocked off at either end—almost an extension of the tearoom itself, only with nothing but some sheet metal as a roof. Some men stood guard at the other end and nodded at our group once they saw Mr. Song. He, Mr. Deng, Miss Cai, and Miss Gaunt led us through large, unadorned iron doors into a large warehouse. Inside were a number of crates, mostly empty or containing nothing but shelving, though here and there I spotted weapons racks with a few rifles on them or scattered tin helmets and other accoutrements of war.

Among the crates, we found a figure holding a clipboard and looking about with satisfaction: an older man with gray hair in a side-parting and a neat mustache, as well as austere Chinese clothes in pale green that seemed to be made up of far too much material. The shirt was almost like an apron, and the trousers were almost like skirts. However peculiar the old man might have looked to me, though, he exuded authority and pride, and there was no question he commanded respect. This must have been Mr. Song's father.

He looked around with mild interest as his son went to speak with him. Then he turned to us with a twinkle of amusement in his eye before speaking again to his son. The younger Mr. Song nodded and returned to us.

"This is my father, Song Li-Hwei. Leader of the Viridian Clan and future chief of the International Police Commission. I would advise you to show your respects with a deep bow."

Something in the younger Mr. Song's voice hinted that any disrespect would be unwise, a feeling confirmed by the number of large men in the shadows all around us. I bowed as low as I could.

The leader seemed to be satisfied with our display and walked over to shake hands with us, laughing and pointing at Mr. Scant.

"I've heard about you," he said. "I like you."

Mr. Scant smiled amicably. "I'm glad to hear it."

The leader cleared his throat. "It's good to have visitors. May you follow the path of tranquility and purity always. That is a motto of our group. If I may offer you a truth of the world: he who is held up by the people as a leader has far to fall, but he who pushes the people on from the shadows has nowhere to go but upward."

"Thank you for your wisdom," said Mr. Scant. The leader laughed, tousled Victor's hair, and turned away.

"Let's leave while he's in a good mood," said Miss Gaunt.

Elspeth and Cai's companions led us back into the teahouse, but the table we had crowded around before was now occupied. "I've had enough Chinese tea anyway," said Miss Gaunt. "Let's go for some *gâteaux*."

"Lemon cake?" said Miss Cai.

"Lemon cake," Miss Gaunt confirmed.

A walk of five or six minutes took us to a little cake shop, standing alone at the end of a street. Little replica statues and French flags stuck into plant pots surrounded it. The interior was equally eccentric, with a mishmash of European cultural items, mostly plaster copies of famous statues such as the Venus de Milo and the Boy with Thorn, but also old maps, cuckoo clocks, wooden clogs, and model cats in every corner. Fortunately there were no other customers, because our large group filled the cake shop entirely. A middle-aged French lady greeted us, speaking in French, and Victor brightened considerably as he spoke with her.

I sat with Mr. Scant on one side of me and kept a space for Victor on the other. Opposite me was Mr. Song, with Mr. Deng at his side, and then Miss Cai sat with Miss Gaunt, completing our circle at the shop's lone table. Miss Cai ordered some cakes and a pot of chamomile tea, then let out a satisfied breath.

"There's really no better place to discuss matters than over tea," she said.

"It's certainly something we've been doing a lot," I said.

"Where to start?" said Miss Cai. "Ah, yes! I'm angry with you. You really have no idea, do you, what you've been stumbling into? You should have come straight to us."

"We didn't know where you were," I said.

"Because you didn't read my letter."

"Because we didn't *get* your letter," I countered. "Why didn't you send a telegram?"

"I can't be sure who will read a telegram before it reaches its recipient," Miss Cai said.

"So what have we, ah, stumbled into?" said Mr. Scant. "You mentioned the child emperor."

That was when Miss Gaunt sat forward. She always wore a detached expression, but a trace of anger flared in those pale eyes of hers. I found myself unable to look away.

"As we mentioned before," Miss Gaunt began, "the day after tomorrow, the Xuantong Emperor himself is expected in Shanghai for the Dragon Boat Festival. He will of course be kept well-sheltered on the royal barge, but there will be a great crowd.

We are not certain, but we suspect the reason a number of young men from France have gone missing is that they will be here, dressed in military uniforms and ordered to march on the emperor. They won't reach him, but it won't matter. That will be enough to begin a new war, a war that will unite the people against the foreigners once more—and perhaps against the emperor first. Hundreds will die that day, thousands more in the war to come. And once the war begins, societies like the Star and Stone Association will keep order over the people, shaping the new China. We mean to stop them."

"Stop what?" said Mr. Scant. "The march? The plot? You say the Star and Stone Association is behind it. I'm sure you're aware I met with them."

"Of course we know," said Miss Cai. "That bungler from Scotland Yard is trying so hard to find out what's going to happen, but he's grasping in the dark."

"They had weapons," Mr. Scant said. "Enough for a small army."

"Yes," said Mr. Deng. "Weapons for a plan like this one."

"We have to stop them," I said. "Mr. Scant, we have to help."

"I'm not sure it's our business," said Mr. Scant.

"And I'm not sure whom we should trust. One secret society tells us to help it stop another."

"The Viridian Clan is not a group of simple criminals," said Miss Cai. "We are working with a union of twelve governments to form a joint international police commission. That includes approval from the emperor himself."

"May I divine from your phrasing that this is still only a plan and there is, as yet, no international police force?" Mr. Scant asked.

"Oh, you are so infuriating!" Miss Cai said with a directness that took me aback.

The younger Mr. Song, who had been sitting in silence, leaned forward diplomatically. "Until it is demonstrated that countries and empires will benefit from cooperation, nobody wants to risk being associated with a failed experiment. But know that while secret societies hope to remain secret, this is not our intention."

Mr. Scant straightened. "What has brought this country to the brink of revolution has been the failure of different countries to work together in peace. Yet you want to make a police force that depends on countries cooperating?"

The shop's kind-faced middle-aged lady broke

the tension, coming with our cakes and tea. Victor was with her, and proudly said, *"Regardez!"* as he pointed to a bicorn hat boasting a small cockade with the French flag on one side—clearly a gift from the shopkeeper. Mr. Scant and his niece regarded each other in frosty silence as the owner laid out her cakes, narrating what was what in lilting French, and then curtseyed before she withdrew.

Mr. Scant began distributing cakes, so I decided to end the silence.

"Are the Tri-Loom involved in this plan to attack the emperor?"

"No matter how much intelligence we gather, it's hard to know *what* the Tri-Loom are involved with," said Mr. Song. "But it's likely they were the ones active on the streets of Paris. Rounding up young men and bringing them to China against their will. We are not certain why they have chosen France. Perhaps some contacts here in the French Concession made it possible. What we know is that there are dozens of the young Frenchmen, probably around two hundred."

"So Victor's brother may be one of them?" I said.

"Eh?" Victor almost dropped his mille-feuille. "Brother? Julien?"

"*Peut-être*," I said—perhaps—and Victor began to listen intently, crumbs around his mouth.

"We don't know the details of the Star and Stone Association's plan," said Miss Cai. "But we are treating this as a test. There are a lot of eyes on us from around the world, and we'll be doing our utmost to protect the emperor—*and* any other victims of their plan."

"And while we have a certain confidence in our power to stop this happening," Elspeth said, "help in any form is welcome."

"I'm not sure it's our business," said Mr. Scant. "My priority is still returning you home."

Miss Gaunt did not waver. "It was not you I was asking." And then she looked at me, her eyes looking, for the first time, awake—awake and hopeful and expectant.

"If nothing else, Mr. Scant, we can't abandon Victor's brother," I said. "We have to help if we can. And I think I have a plan."

XI

Stars and Stones

AS I saw it, the one clear advantage we could offer Miss Gaunt and her allies was a way back into the Star and Stone Association stronghold. The Viridian Clan needed a means of entering the lair under the bridge, and for that, simply walking up to the door under the bridge and knocking wouldn't get them far. The Star and Stone had to have a reason for opening its door, and I had a hunch we could make that happen.

At the clubhouse, we found Mr. Jackdaw had checked out of his room and left in a hurry, which struck me as highly suspicious. We left Victor sleeping in our room but locked him inside, hopefully safe and sound. Then, on the Bund, we found the Peking-Shanghai Bank remained evacuated, now the site of a crime scene investigation by the local police. We infiltrated the bank behind the backs of two officers busy rolling their cigarettes. Following that, we approached a walkway up above the large bell-shaped hall where the dragon's smoke had been released. Even though four men stood watch around the little statuette, large wooden beams supported the building's domed roof, so we could easily position ourselves directly above the desk where all the panic had started. Then it was a simple matter of Mr. Scant using the thin rope spooled inside his claw, dropping down silently, and snatching the dragon statue from the desk before disappearing upward.

The men who had been rolling cigarettes were back on their guard when we returned, so we couldn't escape the bank the same way we had entered. But from the upper part of the building, we found a window from which we could climb down the ostentatious ornamentation of the building. I did my best to follow Mr. Scant's movements, but my reach was too short. In the end, he took me on his back.

There was nothing more to be done that night, and much for our new allies to prepare, so after going through the plan several times with the Viridian Clan, Mr. Scant and I readied ourselves for an early bed. The white sheets and wispy flower paintings of the lodgings seemed surreal in their normalcy, far too plain and simple after everything I had seen.

"This isn't how I expected things to be," I said. "I think I've had enough secret societies to last a lifetime."

"We should have just taken the girl home whether she liked it or not," Mr. Scant grumbled.

"But then we wouldn't be helping Victor," I said, looking back at him sleeping with one arm hanging over the edge of the bed. "It's important to me."

"I know, Master Oliver. But please don't blame me if this all goes badly wrong."

When we gathered on the iron bridge the next day to put my plan into action, I fancied that Miss Gaunt and Miss Cai were regarding me with a new air of respect. Half a year ago, they had been in England and saw me in some very strange situations as I tried to find out the truth about Mr. Scant. I certainly wanted them to see that I had learned a lot as his apprentice. By their side, Mr. Song leaned nonchalantly against the bridge's handrail, whistling a tune that might have been a nursery rhyme or, for all I could tell, a national anthem.

"Are the rest ready and in position?" asked Mr. Scant.

"They are," said Miss Cai. "Deng's with them."

"Do we have the numbers?"

Miss Cai nodded. "More than enough. Are you sure this will work?"

"No," Mr. Scant said. "But I can improvise."

Miss Cai put her hand on Mr. Scant's shoulder, drawing him closer. "Just so we're clear, you're useful to us now, but I would rather you not be here."

Mr. Scant gave Miss Cai's hand a withering look until she removed it. "One of the few things we can agree on," he intoned.

"If you take the life of a single one of my countrymen in there," Miss Cai continued, "I will hold you accountable not only by the law of this land but of its underworld too."

Mr. Scant regarded her for a moment, as though to see if she was serious. Then he looked back to the door. "I'm confident I can deal with them without killing them."

Miss Gaunt had a long traveling cloak, which she gave to Mr. Scant. It looked strange over his morning coat, but he donned it nonetheless. I was already wearing the entirely black clothes Miss Cai had supplied, which were in a Chinese style because that was what was readily available. In addition to that, I donned a simple black cap to cover my hair, and we tied a dark kerchief around my face.

"I thought you would stop me going in with you," I said to Mr. Scant.

"It's your plan, and I respect it," said Mr. Scant. "You're my apprentice, and by now, if you get into a scrape, you ought to be able to at least protect yourself until I come to rescue you."

"Are you so sure it won't be *me* rescuing *you*?"

Mr. Scant smirked at that, as he tied the cloak. "Yes, I am."

After some final checks, we moved toward the door under the bridge. Mr. Scant assumed his position, I ducked down under his travel cloak, and he knocked in a strange rhythm on the door. I could see nothing from under the cloak, but a second later, I heard the scrape of a metal door panel being pulled open. Mr. Scant stiffly said some Chinese words he had memorized but didn't understand, and then came a short, terse response from the man at the door. There was a long pause, during which I assumed Mr. Scant had produced the dragon statue, and then the hatch was slid shut. The sound of bolts sliding followed, and the heavy door swung open. A moment later, we were on the move.

The space beyond the door was a void of darkness, and that was to our advantage. As a Star and Stone man led Mr. Scant through the passageway, I slipped out from under the traveling cloak and behind the doorman's stool. I carefully watched how the doorman closed and locked the door, but there didn't seem to be anything special about the bolts. Although opening the main door required a large key, the man left it in the keyhole. I tucked myself into the corner and made sure to stay well-hidden until I sensed the man was seated again.

My part in this plan was small. Mr. Scant's was much larger. I strained to hear him but I could not. Inside the Star and Stone Association's lair, there was a lot of noise—chatter and laughter and the clinking of what sounded like teacups and crockery. In one hand, I gripped tightly the tin can I had brought in with me. In the other hand, I rolled the single match I had been given between my fingers, then scrambled to pick it up again when I dropped it.

Mr. Scant would be deep inside by now, with the Star and Stone leaders, showing them the dragon. It didn't particularly matter what he said to them. The point was to give them a taste of their own medicine. As long as Mr. Scant stayed safe, everything would work out well.

I heard the commotion before the man in the chair did. Distant angry voices and shouts. I struck the match on the ground and dropped it into the tin can. It immediately began to hiss, and I put it behind me, but by then the doorman was distracted by the noise coming from inside the lair.

I tripped him with my legs, perhaps a little too enthusiastically—my shins would definitely be bruised in the morning. The man fell forward with a cry of alarm, but I was already an arm's length away from him, unbolting the door. One bolt needed to be pushed in before it slid open, but that part wasn't too tricky. I turned the key, and the door swung open just as the man prepared to launch himself at me. Luckily, the young Mr. Song and the others were waiting and poured through the door.

The flare I had lit was filling the passage with thick black smoke, and by then, Mr. Scant had likely done the same in the association's inner chamber. Mr. Song dragged the doorman onto his chair while dozens of men from the Viridian Clan pushed their way inside and into the headquarters of their rivals.

The doorman struggled and yelled, but Mr. Song and I tied his wrists with the rope I had tucked into my belt. Then Mr. Song patted me on the shoulder and we headed inside.

The Stars and Stone Association had been taken by surprise, and its ranks were easily overwhelmed. Some brutal fighting still took place in certain corners of the inner chamber, with tables upturned and bowls of rice smashed on the ground, but the men in green had the upper hand. The room had originally been a storehouse, but the association had converted it into some kind of gambling den, with a number of flags crudely attached to the brick walls, along with some vulgar posters. Miss Cai and Miss Gaunt were stopped in their tracks by a big man with a long stringy mustache, but Miss Gaunt quickly blew something in his eyes, and then Miss Cai was behind him, kicking at the back of the man's knees so that his legs buckled and he fell.

Hurrying past the fighting, Mr. Song and I found another corridor, leading deeper into the subterranean space, where the smoke was far thicker. I knew that was where Mr. Scant would be. Hearing the sound of metal against metal, I rushed in and, through the smoke, could dimly make out two figures locked in combat. The silhouettes charged at one another, and I could discern the claw, flashing out against a sword of some sort, twisting and jerking upward until Mr. Scant had disarmed his opponent.

Miss Cai and Miss Gaunt hurried up behind me. "Is it safe?" asked Miss Cai.

"I think so. Mr. Scant?"

The silhouette took shape as Mr. Scant came closer, his scarf covering half of his face. "Mr. Yau won't be a problem for you."

"And the weapons?"

"Inside."

Miss Cai nodded and called on some men to accompany her. Pulling kerchiefs up over their mouths and trying in vain to wave the flare smoke away from their faces, they vanished into the room beyond so rapidly it was as though they had fallen into a hole.

Mr. Scant didn't look happy. "Yau"—who must have been the man he'd disarmed—"didn't answer any of my questions. Only ranted about his destiny as true ruler of China. I feel as though we're meddling in things that are none of our business."

"I just want to help Victor," I said.

"Helping the boy is one thing. Helping secret societies steal guns from one another is quite another."

"One wants to hurt the young emperor," I said as if it weren't clear, "and the other is a kind of police service."

"Hmm," Mr. Scant said, and left it at that.

We went outside to wait. I took the kerchief off my face, and Mr. Scant removed the travel cloak. Before long, men in green started to appear with boxes and small crates, concealing rifles with their sheets or jackets, the weapons obvious to us but probably not conspicuous to anyone who should chance upon the scene. Miss Cai and Miss Gaunt soon appeared too, uncovering their faces. Miss Cai smiled triumphantly.

"It's a great thing you've done today," she said. "There's plenty of evidence here that they were planning something well beyond the selling of arms. We'll get confessions out of them. And we've confiscated the guns, so the attack cannot go ahead. All that's left is to find where they've got the young Frenchmen, but I promise we'll make them talk soon enough."

"Victor will be happy," I said. "We should go and get him." We hadn't told a soul, not even our allies, but that morning we had left Victor in the care of the nice lady baker in the French Concession who had given him his latest hat.

"Does this mean you'll be coming home with us?" Mr. Scant asked his niece.

Miss Gaunt sighed. "Once we find the missing citizens and I have given my report, yes, I will come back to England with you. There are people I need to talk to in Britain about the International Police Commission, in any case."

"You'd better write a lot while you're away," said Miss Cai.

"I will."

"More than you write to your parents." Miss Cai looked to us. "You should take some time to relax and enjoy the city. Tomorrow's festival will be happy and safe, thanks to you. If you haven't seen it yet, may I suggest the Jing'an Temple? Any rickshaw driver will take you there."

"Your recommendation is appreciated," said Mr. Scant. "We'll get out of your way."

"Thank you for all your help," said Miss Cai. "I mean that. It was a good plan, Master Diplexito. You must be happy it went so well."

"I'll be happy when we find Victor's brother," I said.

"We will," said Miss Cai.

When we returned to the bakery in the French Concession, we found Victor lying flat on one of the benches, rubbing his belly and groaning softly. Even though it was not yet noon, he had apparently gorged himself with cakes. Mr. Scant explained to him that his brother had not been found yet, but that they had caught the person who had taken him away, who would soon reveal Julien's whereabouts. Victor nodded happily and lay back down.

Mr. Scant was quiet that afternoon. We did go to see the temple, where, for a silver tael or two, a friendly young monk took us on a tour of the large and extravagant site. Our guide delighted Victor by pointing out all the little animal carvings up on the roof and taking us to see the statues of the Buddha, whose expression filled me with an odd mixture of tranquility and foreboding. Mr. Scant said almost nothing during the tour, looking with suspicion into every corner or at every passerby, and elsewise seeming lost in thought.

The evening that followed passed calmly, though Victor kept asking for news of his brother. However, no word came from Miss Cai or Miss Gaunt, and in the end, it became apparent there would be no further contact that day. Though I thought I would be too worried to sleep, I began to doze much sooner than I expected, and changed into my bedclothes unaided before getting into bed early.

"Perhaps that's that," I said, aloud, and smiled to myself before settling into the pillows to sleep.

Some hours later, well before morning, I was shaken awake by a wild-eyed Miss Cai, which admittedly didn't come as a surprise whatsoever.

"What's happened?" I said, rubbing my eyes.

"Something's wrong," said Miss Cai, glancing anxiously back at Mr. Scant, who stood behind her. "There's been some kind of fight at the Songs' house. Nobody knows where they are, father or son."

"Forgive us for waking you," said Mr. Scant. "It seemed urgent."

"I don't mind." I thought for a moment and then looked at Miss Cai. "Why did you come to us?"

"I . . ." That question seemed to take her by surprise. "Elspeth and Shu-Ming—Mr. Deng—are already out searching. Some members of the Viridian Clan are helping but most are guarding the teahouse in case of reprisals from the Star and Stone."

"Do you think they're behind this?"

"Of course!" Miss Cai said. "I don't know how they found out where the Songs live, but they must have done it."

"Okay. Let me get dressed. We'll help."

Miss Cai nodded and turned to take her leave, but Mr. Scant stopped her. "Just one thing," he said. "Were there any answers about these French captives?"

"I heard one of the Star and Stone *hongmen* say something about the warehouses by the North Railway Station. But I don't know if it was true."

As Miss Cai commenced to wait outdoors and Mr. Scant helped me to dress, I asked him, "Where should we go, the station or Mr. Song's house?"

"Neither," said Mr. Scant. "It's clear to me there's only one place we should go, and that is the Hu Bao Tea House."

Outside the clubhouse, Miss Cai looked at Mr. Scant as though he were an idiot. "Why the teahouse? I was there earlier—just after the word of the attack on the Songs' home."

"There are some things we need to make certain of," Mr. Scant replied.

"What things?"

"It will be easier to show you."

At that, I gave her a soft, hopefully disarming smile. "We'll need you."

Miss Cai looked at Victor, who had stepped up beside me with determination on his face. "Is it safe for the little one?"

"We'll look after him," I said. "If there's a chance we'll find his brother today, he deserves to be here."

We left the clubhouse as a party of four, so a rickshaw was too small for our trip to the teahouse, and instead we took a cab. Miss Cai shook her head as we alighted. "This is where I started this morning," she said. "Why are we here?"

"*Because* it's where you started," said Mr. Scant. "And where none of you intended to return during your search."

"Zhao-Ji! Oliver!"

I turned to look who had called to us, but really, there was only one person I knew who could call out at the top of her voice yet still sound completely uninterested. Miss Gaunt was hurrying toward us. Miss Cai stepped toward her with a frown on her face. "Why are you here?" she said.

"I assume you came to the same conclusion as I did," said Miss Gaunt. "But how will we get in?"

"Conclusion? What conclusion?" asked Miss Cai.

"They won't just let us inside, of course. Good morning, Uncle."

"Elspeth," Mr. Scant said with nod. "You realized where to come, I see."

"Are you all mad?" said Miss Cai. "What are we doing here?"

"Isn't it obvious?" I said. "The Songs can't be found because they're in a place you haven't been looking. A place well-guarded and newly stocked with guns . . ."

Realization crossed Miss Cai's face, but she shook her head in disbelief. "You think it's . . . ? No. I won't believe it." She stalked toward the entrance of the tearoom but was pushed away by a pair of Viridian Clan members guarding the door. An angry exchange in Chinese ensued.

"Why won't they let you in?" I asked.

"They say they've been ordered to keep everyone out, but they don't know why."

"Can we use the alleyway behind the teahouse?" Mr. Scant asked.

"They'll expect it," said Miss Gaunt. "And these guards will be raising the alarm as soon as we leave."

"So the only way—" Mr. Scant began.

"—is a frontal assault," Miss Gaunt finished for him, then called out, "Down, Zhao-Ji!"

Miss Cai had trained herself thoroughly, so where others may have looked back or asked for clarification, she dropped down low without hesitation. Mr. Scant was already throwing something, which hit one man at the door on the forehead and sent him staggering. It was a smoke bomb of some sort. Mr. Scant was a great believer in smoke bombs.

As the projectile rebounded from the man's skull, Mr. Scant kicked it like a sportsman, which seemed to me a most peculiar action for him. Miss Gaunt dipped and pulled out some manner of small club or cosh from her boot, which she used to upend the other doorman in one neat, precise motion.

I walked behind the others, holding Victor's shoulders protectively. As Mr. Scant and Miss Gaunt stepped into the teahouse, closely followed by Miss Cai, who was drawing out a cosh of her own, the room erupted into chaos. The Viridian Clan rose up against its own and swarmed around Miss Cai, as well as the rest of us, but Mr. Scant had his claw on his hand and was in no mood for gentleness. A big man took a swing at him, but Mr. Scant sent him reeling and holding a bloody nose. Miss Gaunt and Miss Cai moved with grace and coordination, clubbing the nearest assailants before stepping back to back so that nobody could sneak up behind them.

Mr. Scant took it upon himself to disarm everyone who stood against him, tripping them or sending them reeling with blows to the head. Remembering my target practice, I picked up some of the rice bowls and teacups that had fallen to the floor and threw them every time I had a clear shot at someone's head. Victor stepped forward several times, wanting to help, but I was careful to push him behind me.

"Onward!" I heard Mr. Scant yelling as he led the girls out into the alleyway. A sound like the cracking of a vast whip came from the door that led into the storeroom beyond. Mr. Scant ducked instinctively, then threw out another of his smoke bombs, waiting for the initial volley of gunfire to subside before dashing into the alleyway with the others behind him.

The three unlikely allies worked together to quickly overpower the two men who had taken up rifles before they had a chance to reload—Miss Cai throwing her cosh to disorient them before Mr. Scant swiped their weapons away, and Miss Gaunt tripping them to send them to the ground. Another man ran out of the warehouse with a rifle, the door closing quickly behind him, but before he could raise the weapon, Miss Cai surged at him and put his arm into a painful lock.

I ran with Victor into the alley, to seek refuge behind a crate, as there could still be Viridian Clan members behind us, and Miss Gaunt made sure we were safe while Mr. Scant and Miss Cai tried the large, sealed warehouse doors. Mr. Scant reloaded one of the Viridian clansmen's rifles, then handed it to Miss Cai. With his claw, Mr. Scant pried the warehouse door open just enough for her to shoot the wooden bolt holding the door shut. As one, Mr. Scant, Miss Cai, and Miss Gaunt battered the door with their shoulders until the damaged wooden bolt split.

At the moment the door gave, Mr. Scant and the girls jumped aside. A motorcar burst out into the alley, narrowly missing them. I knew the face of the driver—squat, balding Mr. Adams from the bank. The motorcar was hauling a wagon behind it, covered in tarpaulin and tipping precariously as Mr. Adams, traveling at top speed, rounded the corner out of the alley. Following behind the motorcar was a Triumph motorcycle, and the two vehicles sped straight toward a barricade that kept the alleyway secluded from the main street. The motorcar burst through the barricade and out onto the road beyond, sending cyclists and rickshaws scattering. The motorcycle did not follow it, however. The Triumph skidded to a halt at the end of the alley, its rider dragging something along the ground so that a fountain of sparks rose up.

The man held a sword with a curved blade, and I was momentarily reminded of the first time I saw Mr. Scant fight, back in England, when a man all in black had come into our house to challenge him. But unlike that night, the rider's face was not covered—and it was a face I knew. The elder Mr. Song, the leader of the Viridian Clan, who was supposed to have gone missing. The moment I realized this, Mr. Song raised the sword and began charging toward me and Victor, now on the wrong side of the crate and in a lot of danger.

I urged myself to jump aside and take Victor with me to safety, but at that moment, my legs felt like lead. Instead, it was Miss Gaunt who pulled us out of the path of the motorcycle. Mr. Scant, meanwhile, ran toward the motorcycle with his claw ready to strike.

"We need to get to Mr. Adams," I said to Miss Gaunt as Miss Cai called out to Mr. Song in Chinese. "I'm sure he has the guns in that wagon."

"First we need to deal with Song Li-Hwei," Miss Gaunt said, looking at Mr. Song as he readied the motorcycle for another charge. "We don't have a choice."

"Mr. Scant can deal with him."

"I have to keep you safe until he does."

Until she said those words, I hadn't realized what I needed to do.

"No. You don't," I said. Then I called out, "Mr. Scant! We're going ahead. Deal with this one."

Mr. Scant didn't look at me, but I knew I had his attention. "Do you have a plan?" he asked.

"Yes, Mr. Scant."

"Very well. Then go."

And so, with a nod he could not see, I headed back toward the tearoom, along with Victor and Miss Gaunt. Miss Cai stayed to help Mr. Scant deal with Mr. Song and his motorbike. Although the two of them didn't like one another much, I was confident they would fight well together.

In the teahouse, a number of the men who had been knocked down were recovering, but the fight had gone out of them, and Miss Gaunt's cosh kept the rest at bay. Out on the streets, we looked around for a driver, but there were none. "Where are the cabs?" I asked.

"They don't come into the French Concession," said Miss Gaunt. "We need to go toward the main roads."

"No need to get yourselves worked up, what?" came a familiar voice. My heart sank as I turned around slowly to see Mr. Jackdaw, who bared his strange teeth in that charming grin of his. "Hello, Master Diplexito."

XII

Warehouse D

"Y ou scoundrel!" I shouted. "I *knew* we couldn't trust you when you disappeared. I suppose you're going to hand us over to the Star and Stone."

"Whoa there!" said Mr. Jackdaw, as though I were some misbehaving horse. "I think you have me all wrong. I'm not in league with the Star and Stone, my dear boy."

"You're not?"

"I'm with the Yard and always will be. Now, are we going to chase after that wagon full of guns or not?"

"How can we catch up with the motorcar?" asked Miss Gaunt.

"It's festival day," said Mr. Jackdaw. "Not easy to get through the traffic, but a little easier while cycling. We can weave through the stationary vehicles that way."

He stepped aside to reveal his bicycle, and behind it, one of the local rickshaws, only with a longer front handle, so that he could pull it along while he cycled.

"Will that work?" I asked.

"I have great confidence in my strength. I have been in training." He turned toward Victor. "Perhaps we should leave the little one somewhere out of harm's way."

"No," I said. "It's important he comes. I think we'll need him."

"Are you sure? I won't be able to stay with you all the while."

"I've been training too," I said. "I can protect him, with Miss Gaunt's help."

Miss Gaunt was already stepping into the rickshaw. "We have no time to lose," she said.

"Very true," said Mr. Jackdaw. "Away we go!"

"I . . . I suppose I owe you an apology," I said, once we were in motion. "I'm sorry I misjudged you."

"It's not a bad thing to have a suspicious mind, young Master Diplexito," Mr. Jackdaw replied.

Miss Gaunt was subdued as we began to pick up speed. "I can't understand why Mr. Song is doing this," she said. "He hates the Star and Stone so much. Why would he help them?"

"Perhaps he isn't helping the Star and Stone," Mr. Jackdaw called back. "Perhaps you should consider the Tri-Loom."

"He was going to be chief of the new international police," said Miss Gaunt. "Why would he aid a crime syndicate?"

"I'd like to know that too," said Mr. Jackdaw.

Mr. Jackdaw's powerful legs conveyed us onto a busy road. It was as crowded as he had predicted, but the traffic was in motion nonetheless, and I wondered how far Mr. Adams had gotten in his motorcar. Winding between carriages, motorcars, and rickshaws, we concentrated on trying to spot the big wagon. But as the traditional Chinese streets pushed aside the French buildings, there was no sign of the banker. I felt myself shiver.

"Are you afraid without your Mr. Scant?" Miss Gaunt asked.

"I'm excited," I shouted back. "I feel free. But Mr. Scant isn't far away."

"There's Adams!" cried Mr. Jackdaw. I craned my neck to see but I could not spot the wagon. Still, I could feel Mr. Jackdaw pedal harder, and reflected that if he was doing this much for us, he must have been on our side.

"If you get close, I'll jump across," said Miss Gaunt.

"I'll do my best, ma'am," said Mr. Jackdaw.

Finally, I recognized the wagon, square and solid and entirely stationary in the road. Able to pass between the lines of festival traffic, we were gaining on Mr. Adams fast. Miss Gaunt stood up and began to position herself with one foot braced against the seat of the rickshaw. Though there were dozens of vehicles around us, along with innumerable pedestrians and an assortment of animals too, the wagon began to swell larger and larger in my vision, like a balloon being slowly inflated. Then we were almost upon the banker. I could feel Miss Gaunt begin to coil next to me like a spring.

And then all three of us nearly tumbled out of the rickshaw altogether, as someone led their donkey in front of us and Mr. Jackdaw was forced to brake. "Hurry, confound you!" he yelled at the peasant, who looked back at us with little interest. Unsurprisingly, the moment the way became clear, the traffic began to move again and the wagon went beyond our reach. Worse, Mr. Adams turned away down a side road, his destination apparently not the same as that of the crowds.

"I think he's going to the North Station," said Mr. Jackdaw.

"They said something about the station earlier," I called back.

"I can't keep up!"

Mr. Jackdaw's cycling prowess was not to be understated, but the motorcar was faster than any cyclist, even while towing a wagon, and Mr. Adams soon got away from us once again. But Mr. Jackdaw pedaled on manfully, until finally we reached a kind of bridge with a steep slope downward, leading us toward train tracks and various large buildings.

"This is where they went," said Mr. Jackdaw, breathing heavily after his exertions. "But if I cycle down that way, the rickshaw you're in will get ahead of me, and we'll be in a terrible state. So this is where I'll take my leave of you."

"Take your leave?" I repeated. "Surely you'll come with us?"

"Afraid not, old chap," said Mr. Jackdaw. "I have to go to the river to be sure of a plan B. The emperor's barge will already be in the city, and I mean to see it comes to no harm. The road leads to the railway warehouses, and it should be clear which one they're using. So for now, *bon chance!*"

We stepped down from the rickshaw, and Mr. Jackdaw disentangled himself from it, doffed his cap, and was gone. The rickshaw lay crookedly where it had been left behind, as though a little befuddled by being abandoned—just as I was. "I suppose we're on foot from here," said Miss Gaunt. I took Victor's hand, and we began our descent. The warehouses were in a kind of sunken area, crisscrossed by train tracks. Held above the rest was the immaculate new station building.

I made sure Victor stayed close, but he set a fearsome pace. Perhaps he sensed his brother was near or he had understood enough of what had been said to know what awaited us. Somehow, his bicorn hat seemed to give him a greater sense of purpose, and his long hair gave him the look of a child from one of those revolutionary paintings. He peered up at me, then gave me a nod and a wide grin.

We saw Mr. Adams's motorcar outside a warehouse marked with the letter *D*. It was a large structure, with its only windows placed very high up and no apparent way in other than through the large doors through which the motorcar was passing. There was no chance of slipping in that way unseen, so we set about looking for any other points of entry, finally discovering a rudimentary ladder up to the roof.

Having climbed the ladder, we first checked if any guards were waiting for us on the rooftop. Satisfied that they were not, Miss Gaunt and I took a moment to sort out our plan. This included telling Victor to go back down the ladder alone, which Miss Gaunt conveyed to him in French. He seemed unsure but agreed after some dithering and began to climb down. Miss Gaunt and I then turned our attentions to a locked doorway, horizontal along the flat rooftop.

"How do we deal with the lock?" she asked.

"Leave it to me," I said, and set to work. It was a lock of a newer sort, with a number of bolts to align before the barrel would turn, but I could feel when each was in place, so finding the alignment was not so difficult. Once the key turned and the door came open, Miss Gaunt peered inside the space cautiously, but I said, "No need for stealth."

"True enough," said Miss Gaunt.

"Is anybody there?" I called down the stairs, which might have seemed like a foolish thing to do, but our plan required we get the attention of anyone who might be guarding the building. When no one below responded, we stepped into the doorway and made our way down the iron steps. At the bottom of the stairwell, there was a kind of office with a view out over the main floor of Warehouse D. Through this office window, I saw the French soldier boys for the first time. They were lined up along the warehouse floor, standing in front of horse-drawn wagons. A member of the Viridian Clan distributed rifles to them, and then each boy boarded the wagon nearest to him.

The door of the office shut behind me and Elspeth, and a figure stepped out of the darkness behind it. "An impressive sight, no? And all the better for the guns you helped supply." The younger Mr. Song seemed very pleased with himself as he raised a revolver.

"Yu-Sheng?" said Miss Gaunt. "You're part of this too? You're . . . putting the Tri-Loom above the Viridian Clan or the police project? You said an international police was your dream."

"A dream, yes," Mr. Song said, as more men came up the stairs behind us, armed with swords or staffs. "But I must be sure China is still a nation when it happens. The rest of the world wants to tear us to pieces. This part goes to the English, this part to the French, the Germans, the Dutch, the Japanese.

And then, when there's nothing left of China but the Forbidden City, *then* where is our place in an international police? First, we must preserve China. And to do that, we must expel the foreigners. The only way to do it is to turn my countrymen, united, against them. And what better way to begin than have one of Europe's countries attack the emperor?"

"So you try to use these French boys you've kidnapped? They'll never help you."

"Oh, but they will," the younger Song replied. "Each of these boys has someone he'll do anything to protect, someone who means far more to them than anything they will see here. And they know firsthand we have agents in France. With that threat over their heads, it only takes a little to motivate them."

"The French government will denounce the attack," Miss Gaunt said. "They'll say it wasn't their command."

"And we'll be here to call them liars. Who do you think my countrymen will believe? China will regain the strength our ancestors had. Strength enough to defeat any of the other nations of the world. That is when an international police can come into being, underpinned by the strength, intelligence, and influence of the true *hongmen*, the men of the Tri-Loom.

Only through them can this dream become reality. And the only people with a chance to stop this are your friends, who Father will deal with, and the two of you. But here you are."

"What about Deng?" said Miss Gaunt. "Did he know about this?"

"Deng's a fool who knows nothing. He'll be clawing through the pieces of our home, out of the way. If only you two were there with him, things would have been so much easier."

"You're forgetting someone," I said. "Three of us came here."

Mr. Song's eyes widened. "The boy." He gave his gun to the man next to him. "Take them alive," he said. "We need to make an example of them later. But if they give you trouble, shoot the girl."

Mr. Song swept past us, hurrying down the stairs to the warehouse floor. The man who had been given the gun leveled it, so Miss Gaunt and I slowly raised our hands. Another man in the office put down his staff and produced a rope, obviously meaning to tie us up, and said something in Chinese to Miss Gaunt. She frowned at him, and he repeated it, more angrily, clearly telling her to lower her hands and put them behind her back. She kept pretending she didn't know what he meant—that was when he went to grab her wrist.

Faster than a scorpion's sting, she clutched the man's wrist first, twisting it up behind his back and stepping behind him so that the group's gunman would shoot his comrade if he fired the rifle. But Miss Gaunt did not want a standoff and instead shoved her captive at the man with the gun, wrongfooting him. I used the moment of surprise to snatch the discarded staff and swing it around at the man with the gun, hitting him hard on the elbow and making him drop the rifle.

The other men gave cries of alarm, and the one with the fastest reaction swung a sword down at Miss Gaunt. She stepped into the attack and tackled the man to the ground. I heard a gunshot and winced, but by then, Miss Gaunt was the one with a revolver in her hand.

Having fired her warning shot, Miss Gaunt pointed the gun at each of the men in sequence. They backed off, the tables turned. I went to her side. "Down the steps," she said.

I did as Miss Gaunt had told me, and she followed behind me, closing the office door behind her. No sooner had we done this than we heard the roar of a motorcycle engine. The younger Mr. Song disappeared out of the main entrance, followed by all the wagons full of false French soldiers. We made our way down to the warehouse floor, Miss Gaunt careful to cover us with her revolver.

"They'll come down the ladder, to cut us off from the outside," I said. Miss Gaunt nodded, looking to the open exit. Around us were the traces of the people who had been living here, most likely for some time— vats of rice gruel, discarded cups and bowls, blankets, and, of course, buckets I didn't want to go anywhere near. Following on foot would be meaningless now, so our only chance was to pursue Mr. Song in a vehicle. There was only one remaining—the motorcar Mr. Adams had used to haul the weapons here.

"Can you drive it?" I asked Miss Gaunt.

"I've never tried. You?"

"Only in Father's engines outside his factory," I said. "Never on any real roads." Miss Gaunt didn't have anything more to say at that. "It has to be me, doesn't it?" I continued. "Bother."

Miss Gaunt cranked the engine as I prepared myself for the hardest part, which was getting the thing in motion at all. I had never understood well how a motorcar's gears worked, but I could at least identify the one gear for starting the thing, so I shifted the big stick into place. After several bumpy starts, I got the thing moving, and Miss Gaunt climbed in beside me. The men from the Viridian Clan formed a blockade across the front entrance, but Miss Gaunt shot at them, and they dived for cover.

"Where am I going?" I said, as the motorcar shuddered into life.

"Follow the tracks."

Thankfully, this motorcar was heavier and slower than Father's engines, so it wasn't as terrifying to drive. Until, of course, we reached the road itself. I couldn't help myself from a few "crikeys" and even a "Gordon Bennett" as I narrowly avoided crushing smaller vehicles or ramming into horses. Luckily, traffic continued to move slowly because of the festival, and I knew that the French youths in their soldiers' uniforms couldn't have gotten far either. On the other hand, Mr. Song could have easily sped past the slow-moving traffic in his motorcycle. As I drove, I hoped Victor had done his part in the plan and had hidden himself well afterward.

Miss Gaunt directed me to the riverfront, and once we saw the crowds, we knew it was time to disembark. "There they are!" she cried, pointing into the distance, and I saw the tops of the wagons.

Now on foot, we began to push our way through the crowds. There were so many people around that Miss Gaunt and I struggled to stay together. She grabbed my hand and pulled me on, yelling at the citizens to get out of our way. We barged past Asian and European and American strangers, protests and curses in a dozen or more languages ringing in our ears.

As we drew close, someone stepped out into our path, yelling, "*Stop!*"

I ran into Miss Gaunt's back and very nearly fell. As I regained my composure, I saw the younger Mr. Song ahead of us, holding up one hand. His other hand was conspicuously hidden behind the small, quavering figure of Victor. I didn't have to see behind my young friend to know Mr. Song had a gun pointed at his back.

"Honestly," said Mr. Song. "This is why the Viridian Clan will never be enough. I ask them to do one simple thing, keep you busy, and they couldn't even manage that. Hand over your gun, please. Hand it over. Good. Fortunately for you, I found your little friend before he could get to his brother."

He held Victor by the collar, his other hand still pointed at the little boy's back, and led us to a where

Mr. Adams was waiting, up on a small platform that on an ordinary day might have been a bandstand. Mr. Song nodded, and Mr. Adams waved a red flag. Beyond the platform's edge, I could see the scale of the miniature French army. There must have been two hundred young men there, or very nearly, and they had begun to march.

The Frenchmen had no true military training, so they did not keep ranks well, nor march in unison. But—advancing unstoppably—they still looked formidable. Onlookers began to notice them and many cleared a path, but at a certain point, the crowd became too thick, and none of the festivalgoers could move. As the young men approached this cluster, a series of loud bangs sounded off, one after another, like a bonfire collapsing in on itself. Somebody screamed.

"Yes," said Mr. Song. He began to look for the onslaught's first victims but frowned when it became clear there were none. "A warning shot?" he said. Mr. Adams was frowning too. However, the crowd had taken notice of the gunfire, and panic was beginning to spread. The false army advanced.

After a few dozen paces, the Frenchmen stopped again, and this time their action was clear. Almost in unison, the men aimed their guns into the sky and fired. Plumes of smoke rose upward, ghosts of little dragons ascending together.

"What are they doing?" demanded Mr. Song. Victor looked back to me and grinned.

The young Frenchmen reached the riverbank, where I now saw many boats had amassed, including a huge golden barge that must have belonged to the emperor. One man stepped forward, and though I could only see him from the back, I knew he would have a face that was bruised and bloodied, following a recent beating.

"Julien!" Victor cried out.

We could not hear what Julien said, and I doubt I could have understood his French at any rate, but his gestures and tone made his meaning clear—France was paying tribute to China and wished the emperor eternal happiness. Or something along those lines. The men shot in the air one more time and then kneeled, heads bowed, like the knights of old.

"Julien!" Victor yelled again, but Mr. Song tossed him aside.

"Prepare the bomb," said Mr. Song. Mr. Adams nodded and slipped away.

The younger Mr. Song kept us pressed to the handrail of the little platform but moved around us so that he could see the river. His eyes were fixed on the royal barge. A moment later, we heard a whistling sound. A large firework exploded far above our heads, like a huge green flower, and although it was still daytime—and the effect would have been far more impressive at night—the firework was powerful enough to light up the sky. A brief series of secondary fireworks went off around it, and laughter and applause erupted from the crowd. I looked at the golden barge, and while I saw no movement on it, I did spot a smaller barge beside the boat. A short figure dressed in finery danced excitedly on the smaller craft, before a rotund adult urged the child back out of sight.

"What is this?" Mr. Song roared, but there was nobody to listen to him. Mr. Adams had disappeared. And so he turned to us in his fury. "What did you do?"

"You may have stopped Victor from reaching his brother," I said, "but he still reached the other French boys and spread a message. It doesn't matter if you beat them, starved them, locked them away—now they've seen the threat to their families and loved ones wasn't real. I'm sure that set a lot of them thinking. Victor even suggested this little tribute himself."

Mr. Song rubbed a hand over his mouth. Then he pulled out the revolver he had taken from Miss Gaunt. "You're so clever, you've gotten yourselves killed," he said.

He didn't see the shape rise up behind him, the shape that swung a wooden beam at his head so hard it splintered upon contact. Mr. Song was knocked to the ground and didn't move.

"Thank you, Mr. . . ." I began, and then blinked. "Mr. Deng."

"You're welcome," said Mr. Deng. "Sorry to disappoint you—I suppose you were expecting your butler."

"No, I'm very happy to see you."

"Did you hear all of that?" said Miss Gaunt, looking from Mr. Song to Mr. Deng.

"Enough," Mr. Deng said. "And to think I trusted him. The whole clan must have known about this, apart from me and Zhao-Ji."

"Where is Miss Cai?" I asked. "And Mr. Scant?"

As it had transpired, Mr. Scant was at the riverside with Julien. "Ah, there you are," he said as we arrived. With a loud cry, Victor ran to embrace his older brother, running around him and chattering away like a pet ferret happy to see its owner. All around us, the young Frenchmen were dancing and celebrating with the locals as though the whole thing were an arranged party.

"I was about to come and make sure you were alright," Mr. Scant added.

"Thanks to Mr. Deng," I said. "Were you worried about me?"

"You're my apprentice," said Mr. Scant. "I should hope by now you've learned to keep yourself alive."

"Did you set off the fireworks?" I said. "I don't know where those came from."

"Well, I helped a little. But I didn't have the time to set anything off. The older of the Songs proved to be a most formidable opponent. I prevailed only thanks to a most splendid throw by Miss Cai, catching the old man on the back of the head at just the right moment. She has him restrained and is trying to figure out what to do with him. Until today, Mr. Song was the person she would have gone to with a prisoner, as it would happen."

"So who did you help?"

"Me, of course," Mr. Jackdaw said, appearing from behind Mr. Scant. "Incidentally, I'd say I'm also the person who ought to take custody of our Mr. Song. And Mr. Song Junior, to boot. I had a bit of time left over after dismantling rather a large bomb, and I thought it would be nice to contribute something to the local celebrations, what? Unlike you, I didn't really have the means to stop a small French army, so this was my modest contribution. Now, would you be so kind as to lead me to Miss Cai's prisoner?"

In high spirits, we walked back through the crowds toward the small park where Miss Cai would be waiting for us with the restrained elder Mr. Song. Mr. Deng followed us, with the younger Mr. Song on his shoulder. The display drew some odd looks from passersby, but nobody made any comment.

"This is it," Mr. Scant said as we reached the park's entrance. The grounds were surprisingly quiet, given the nearby crowds, but I supposed everyone was watching the festivities at the river.

"Wait," I said. "Isn't that . . .?"

I didn't need to finish my sentence. We had forgotten about Mr. Adams, and there he was, across the park, slipping away.

"He'll have freed Song," said Mr. Scant. "This is bad." With a look at Miss Gaunt and Mr. Jackdaw, he began to run, with the rest of us close behind.

XIII
The Message

Song, though free of his restraints, did not run from us. In fact, he was waiting calmly as we reached the open courtyard at the center of the park. The courtyard had stone tables with chessboards built into them, and he was inspecting the pieces with his back to us. Slumped on the table across from him, as though she had fallen asleep whilst playing a game with Mr. Song, was Miss Cai. Blood pooled around her head, running down onto the floor beneath her.

Mr. Adams was whispering in Mr. Song's ear, and then, with a fearful look at us, he crept away. "I'll go for him," Mr. Jackdaw said, and set off in pursuit, giving the elder Song a wide berth.

"Zhao-Ji!" called Miss Gaunt. "Are you all right?"

"I would not describe her as all right. Nor is she

dead," Mr. Song said in an uninterested tone. "She would make a poor bargaining chip if she were."

"Bargain?" said Miss Gaunt. "If you've hurt her, there won't be any bargaining, Song Li-Hwei, mark my words."

That made Mr. Song turn around for the first time, with a look of amusement. "You won't call me *shīfu* anymore? I am no longer your teacher? I suppose I deserve no less. But Cai Zhao-Ji is hurt already. She is hurt badly. Yet still you will bargain with me, because she is still alive, and you want her back. And I want my son—and safe passage for us out of China.

"The Tri-Loom won't overlook my failure here," he continued, "and they do not forgive easily. We should never have joined, but Yu-Sheng, he's so ambitious. And so now, I want the airship you arrived in."

I looked back at Mr. Deng, who had put the younger Mr. Song's feet back on the ground but was still supporting his former friend's unconscious form.

"This isn't a game you can win," said Mr. Scant. "We outnumber you and you have nowhere to go. Even if we accede to all your demands, what prevents us from breaking our word as soon as Miss Cai is in our custody? You don't have your motorcycle to run away with now. I know how you fight, and there are more of us than there ever were before."

Mr. Song placed his hands on his knees. He almost looked like a kindly schoolteacher. "Of course it's too much to hope that your word of honor would be enough." He leaned back and picked up some of the chess pieces, the kings and queens. "Are you familiar with Chinese medicine? We have—what's the word in English? Potions? Tinctures?—that are capable of remarkable things." He held up the red queen. "This, to put an enemy to sleep. She has drunk this one." Next was the red king. "This to waken them."

He unscrewed the crown of the chess piece and shifted to sit beside Miss Cai, before abruptly pulling her upright by her hair. Miss Gaunt stepped forward but hesitated. A deep wound ran down Miss Cai's face, from her forehead and down across the bridge of her nose. The heavy bleeding had stained her face and neck red.

Inside the chess piece was a kind of smelling salt. Mr. Song held it under Miss Cai's nose. She stirred and then winced. She was not really awake but in a kind of daze.

Mr. Song then showed us the white queen. "This one is a poison," he said matter-of-factly. "Fast-acting and debilitating. This, too, she has taken. Here, in the white king, is the antidote. But first, I would have assurances of what I asked for, starting with my son."

A breeze tugged at the trees behind Mr. Song, scattering a few blossoms that danced their way down to the ground.

"She adored you!" Miss Gaunt yelled at Mr. Song.

"And she was an excellent student. In another life, we would have been able to form our international police and do a great good for the world. No longer in our reach, I think."

"You're a monster," I said.

"Not a monster, my boy. No, no. I'm afraid I'm an ordinary man with few choices left. The Tri-Loom will come for me—if not here, anywhere I run to in China, even in your English jail. My only chance is a new start in a new country, for my son first and for myself second. Probably even then we will be found and punished, but it's at least a chance."

"Give her the antidote!" cried Miss Gaunt.

Mr. Song's voice became vicious. "Give me my son and take us to your airship."

"What have you done to me?" came Miss Cai's voice.

"Ah, sweet child," Mr. Song said, letting go of

her hair and even flattening it. "I've given you poison. You are my leverage. I can only thank you."

"I trusted you," Miss Cai managed, opening her eyes with a wrench of effort.

"I know. And you weren't wrong to trust me. If today had been different, we would have gone ahead as we had always planned. We would have become an intelligence network, spanning the whole world—with the Tri-Loom behind it all."

"The Tri-Loom executed my father," Miss Cai growled. With that, she moved, much faster than it had seemed she would be able to. Her hand shot out, and she grabbed the white king from its place on the board. She had unscrewed the crown by the time Mr. Song grabbed the chess piece, but rather than struggle to wrest it from the old man's grasp, she upended it. The antidote spilled out across the ground.

"I will not be your leverage," she growled.

"You lunatic!" Mr. Song cried. But Mr. Scant had taken the moment of distraction to make his move. He charged forward, his claw drawn back, and swiped right at Mr. Song's torso. Mr. Song had seen him coming at the last moment and narrowly escaped the blades, but Miss Gaunt had reached the table too. She hurried Miss Cai to safety, by a nearby bush, as Miss Cai put a finger deep into her mouth, trying to rid herself of the poison she had swallowed.

"Give up," Mr. Scant said to Mr. Song, who had drawn out his knife again. "You have no chance now."

"You mean I have nothing to lose," said Mr. Song. He pulled out one more vial, uncorking it and swallowing it himself. "Another poison, but this one will at least help me take my revenge on you. Ah, I already feel the strength returning to me. Don't think this will be as easy as when you had Cai Zhao-Ji's assistance."

With that, he lunged at Mr. Scant with the knife. Mr. Scant twisted so that the thrust went past his shoulder, and then grabbed Mr. Song by his olive-colored jacket. Mr. Song aimed another stab at Mr. Scant's wrist, forcing him to let go.

Mr. Song continued his offensive with remark-able speed, stabbing again and again in the direction of Mr. Scant's chest, forcing Mr. Scant back, with the claw flashing out again and again to deflect the blows. Whatever Mr. Song had swallowed, it was giving him an abundance of energy, and even Mr. Scant barely had a chance to counterattack. The two circled one another, each man searching for an opening, but whatever Mr. Scant tried, Mr. Song was prepared for him.

Both men were clearly experienced fighters, and they tested one another, trying a number of feints but failing to catch the other man off guard. Mr. Song sidestepped one of Mr. Scant's thrusts and managed to wrap an arm tight around his neck, then pinned Mr. Scant's claw to his hip. For a few long moments they struggled, and Mr. Scant's face began to go red. I knew I had to do something. Without thinking, I stooped to pick up a small stone, and then, remembering all those hours spent practicing my aim, I threw it with all my strength. It flew in a perfect arc, striking Mr. Song on the side of his head and distracting him long enough for Mr. Scant to flip him onto his back. The claw flashed out to pin Mr. Song down, but Song was too fast, rolling away and getting to his feet in an instant.

"He may not have Miss Cai, but he has me!" I called out. Mr. Song met me with only a sneer—but I was not Mr. Scant's only ally. After setting Miss Cai down safely, Miss Gaunt ran to my side, and Mr. Deng stood with us too, having laid Mr. Song's son down behind us. Miss Gaunt had her cosh and gave Miss Cai's to me. I still didn't want to go near

Mr. Song's whirling knife, but holding a cosh was better than being empty-handed. The three of us tried to surround Mr. Song and Mr. Scant, but Mr. Song only grinned and rushed my way. However, that gave Miss Gaunt a chance to strike the old man on the back of his leg, and he stumbled onto one knee. Mr. Deng prepared a mighty punch, but Mr. Scant stopped him.

Whatever concoction Mr. Song had swallowed, it was running out. He was breathing very heavily and didn't seem able to get off his knees. He put one hand on the ground before lowering himself down onto the flagstones. The poison had done its work, and without another word, Mr. Song gave in to its inevitable pull.

The sky had darkened just a little, and from the riverside, fresh fireworks went up, changing the gray flagstones to red and green for a few fleeting moments. After a time, I felt I should speak.

"What should we do?" I said.

"What do you think we should do, Master Oliver?"

"I suppose we need to find Jackdaw and tell him what happened here. And then we'd better go back to Victor and Julien."

"There's something in his hand," I said. The fallen old man held something between his fingertips. "I think it's a business card."

"Whose is it?" asked Miss Gaunt.

I looked at her and then at Mr. Scant. "Someone's written, *Best regards*. But the name . . . It says *Aurelian Binns*."

Epilogue

 the end, we did not return on the airship. Mr. Jackdaw booked passage for himself, Mr. Scant, Miss Gaunt, Miss Cai, Victor, and me on the Orient Express, but learning that Julien would not be traveling with us, Victor refused. A large barge had been arranged for all the young Frenchmen, and so Victor was determined to go by sea. But I sent a telegram to Father, who decided to pay a visit to the French embassy, and in the end, Diplexito Engineering and the French government jointly paid for one hundred and fifty four young Frenchmen to have passage back to Paris by train. This was in fact a smaller number than anticipated, as several of the youths opted to stay in Shanghai to pursue prospects in the French Concession.

The Orient Express was a truly luxurious way

to travel, though a smattering of regular passengers complained that the French boys enjoying their first days of freedom were acting indecorously.

Victor's brother Julien was so grateful when he heard all we had done for Victor that he knelt and tried to kiss our feet, and we had to beg him to stand up again. Victor was the happiest he had ever been. He regaled his brother with tales of hats and Hotchkiss guns and the divine substance that was custard, a wholly different order of foodstuff from *crème anglaise*. Julien, who stood much taller than me and had skin tanned a deep brown, clearly loved his brother dearly. I could tell that the reunion after such a difficult time apart had only brought them closer. At first Julien looked wary, perhaps even envious, when Victor showed me affection, but we soon warmed up to one another.

The journey was not a short one, and Mr. Scant and I devoted a lot of our time to the question of what to do with Victor and Julien. I didn't want to leave Victor behind after becoming so fond of him, and after all, the brothers didn't have a home to go back to. I proposed finding the two of them work at Father's factory, but Mr. Scant suggested one of Father's French contacts might be able to offer a position in Paris. But of course that was before we spoke to the brothers themselves.

Through Miss Gaunt, Victor told me he wanted to be a policeman like Mr. Jackdaw and Mr. Scant—though where he had gotten the impression Mr. Scant was a policeman, we weren't sure. Julien thanked us for our offers of help but said he would look after his brother from now on. Mr. Jackdaw promised he would arrange for lodgings for the boys for three months, during which time Julien could find a job and thereafter pay his own rent. I instructed Mr. Scant to buy them smart new clothes and to leave them with contact details for Father. The brothers agreed and promised they would always try to help other children whose only home was the streets.

"You understand I can't offer the same for the other hundred and fifty-two?" said Mr. Jackdaw.

"I suppose not."

"Are they less deserving because they are not your friends?" Mr. Jackdaw continued. "What about that one boy who helped carried your bags? Does he deserve special attention?"

"I know, I know," I said. "I want to help them all. And I can't—I can't even help one of them, only ask for Father to do it. But after all we've been through together, it really doesn't feel right to leave Victor with nothing."

"What a pity for the other boys, that they didn't get so much time with you."

"It could have worked out much worse for them," I said sadly, to which Mr. Jackdaw just smiled.

Miss Cai was not in good health. Along with her new scar, the poison had taken its toll, and though she hadn't died, the effects were severe. She had developed problems hearing, and her eyesight had deteriorated. Her legs didn't move as she wanted them to either, necessitating use of a wheeled chair. Nobody knew how long the effects could last, and doctors warned her new condition might be permanent.

Nonetheless, she had come to some sort of arrangement with Mr. Jackdaw on the Orient Express, and she had earlier made some contacts in Scotland Yard she now wanted to meet. She seemed excited about the prospect of organizing something new, but felt the best place for herself was with Mr. Jackdaw at the Yard.

As the two of them took their leave of us in Paris, Mr. Jackdaw intoned, "I promise this won't be the last we'll see of one another. I've taken rather an interest in you all and this whole idea of an international police. The Tri-Loom will probably pursue some action in response to your actions in Shanghai, so we'll be sending some men to look after you for a while. From afar, of course. Chin up! The way to deal with powerful enemies is to make even more powerful friends, what?"

He and Miss Cai bade us farewell, Miss Gaunt bowing very deeply to her friend and partner, who she had been tending to every day since Miss Cai's injuries. While her eyes remained dry, Miss Gaunt once again looked as though she were making a thousand different calculations when she raised her head. Miss Cai laughed and beckoned her over for a brisk hug before Mr. Jackdaw wheeled her away down the platform.

Saying good-bye to Victor was difficult. He gave me such a tight hug I couldn't breathe, and everybody laughed. Of course, I gifted him my cap, taking his bicorn hat to remember him by, promising we could swap again any time he came to see us.

During the ferry ride back to England, I kept looking at Aurelian Binns's card. Why had Mr. Song seen fit to produce the card with his last breaths? Was it defiance? A warning? If he and Aurelian had met, what might the two of them have said? There was no way I could know, and when I noticed a little loose part in the corner of the card, pulling at it, I yelped in surprise as the whole calling card incinerated itself.

Back in Tunbridge Wells, Elspeth Gaunt reunited with her father, who was now using a cane to walk about. Uncle Reggie gingerly hugged his daughter, who patted him on the back without much enthusiasm. I thought being reunited with her father would have brought out Miss Gaunt's hidden emotions, but this was not to be. The emotion instead came from her mother, Mrs. Gaunt, who was there too with her cat, Lady Hortensia. She shed tears of joy as she embraced her daughter, squashing the unfortunate cat between them.

Father heard the full account of everything and promised to find Julien work if he needed it. He reprimanded Mr. Scant for being away for so long, as, after all, a man needs his valet, and Mr. Scant apologized sincerely. "It's good things went your way, but we mustn't forget the Binns lad," Father said. "I don't think we'll have heard the last of him."

Mother told me I looked like I'd grown an inch or more and booked me an appointment to have my hair neatened by the barber the very next day.

At dinner, we talked about the idea of an international police force.

"There are some countries that will never trust others," Dr. Mikolaitis said in a low tone.

"It's a fine idea nonetheless," Mother replied, wholly unaware the conversation was not purely hypothetical. "Perhaps something you could be involved in when you're older, Oliver."

"I wonder," I said. "I should certainly like to help others. But I still have so much to learn."

"That's what school is for," said Father. "And that's where you'll be going again, next week. You can regale them all with stories of your travels."

"I'm looking forward to it," I said. "Being so far from home and seeing so many strange things, the main thing I learned was how much I've yet to discover."

I looked at Mr. Scant as I said this. He was in valet mode just then, standing attentively by the door, but he caught my eye as I spoke those words and nodded a slow nod.

"So much more to learn," I said to myself, as I finished my beef and neatly placed my knife and fork onto the center of my plate.

Master
DiPLEXitO and Mr. ScaNt

BOOK III

Mr. Scant must face his past in the third installment of Master Diplexito and Mr. Scant. The thief and his apprentice have caught the attention of powerful new adversaries—enemies who know that even the most upstanding family butler has his secrets!

Old allies and new must come together to protect Scotland Yard as it comes under attack, and this time, Mr. Scant may have to rely on Oliver for protection. Prepare for an adventure that once again takes our intrepid duo far from home—this time, aboard a ship they call "unsinkable" . . .

About the Author

Bryan Methods grew up in a tiny village south of London called Crowhurst. He studied English at Trinity College, Cambridge, and has been working on a PhD on First World War poets. He currently lives in Tokyo, Japan, where he loves playing in bands, fencing, and video games.